Deck
the Shelves

Deck the Shelves

JOELLE CULLEN

J Cullen

LOWER MOUNTAIN

PUBLISHING

Paperback: 979-8-9877818-3-8
Ebook: 979-8-9877818-2-1

Edited by Kristin Avila
Cover Design and Illustration by Melody Jeffries
Formatting by Alt 19 Creative

Lower Mountain Publishing
Printed in the United States of America

First Edition: 2024

www.joellecullen.com

For my children.
Seeing the pure joy
that shines in your eyes
on Christmas morning,
has turned it into my favorite holiday.

CHAPTER ONE

Home for the Holidays
(with a New Friend)

Heartbreak. Job loss. A 'crappy' case of the flu. No matter what the universe throws at you, there's nothing like that restful feeling that blankets you in a big hug when you visit your childhood home.

Stepping inside the walls of 22 Danbury Street instantly released the built-up tension of my real life. The first big inhale of that new-book smell, combined with the cinnamon and vanilla scent of my mother's kitchen, brought a flood of memories that somehow erased any remnants of the day's troubles. Even as I knocked my brolly against the outer bricks of the shop, splashing water down inside my polka-dot wellies, nothing could dampen my spirits.

"We've gone and closed an hour ago, but come in, come in," came the gruff yet friendly greeting from a man stooped over a cardboard box filled with books.

"Always open for dishing out adventures, whether they come from pages or bottles, right, Dad?"

A head popped up from within the box, a face full of gray whiskers and thin spectacles slipping down his nose. "Alice, is that you, dear?" He wiped his hands on his trousers and stepped toward me, engulfing me in a bear hug only Dad could give. He gave me an extra squeeze before letting me go.

"I didn't know we were expecting you. Wait 'til your ma hears. She will be outta her mind trying to cook your favorite dishes without the ingredients on hand." He chuckled, and the wrinkles around his eyes deepened as his smile grew. He turned and shouted, "Honey, come here."

"I know, I know," I replied. "Sheila gave me an unexpected holiday from the marketing firm." This was sort of true, though it was more like my boss ordered a forced exile until I could figure my shite out. No one likes a Debbie Downer in the office around the holidays. "I'll be working from home for a couple of weeks."

"That's just marvelous, my girl. The Christmas season just wasn't the same last year without you." He turned again and yelled up the back stairwell, "Hon, did you hear me? Come on down here!" Turning back to me, he said, "I swear, she can't hear a thing when she's upstairs blasting that stuff she calls music."

I smiled as I heard Mum respond. "Calm down, you old fool. I heard ya. I'm on my way." Ollie and Joyce Evans bickered like children but were the most devoted couple in the village. My father continuously held the door for Mum, even after forty years of marriage, and she always made sure the pantry was stocked with his favorite crisps and his shirts perfectly ironed stiff as a twenty-pound note, just the way he liked them.

"I just couldn't miss the festivities again. I'm so happy to be home for the holidays with you, Mum, and Scarlett. It wasn't nearly the same last Christmas."

Last winter, I had barely kept my head above water, interning with Giles Scott, a famous clothing designer based in London. While I loved every second of catty drama that endlessly filled the space between the racks of clothing in the office, the pressure to be seen and acknowledged required longer hours beyond the nine-to-five hustle. You'd think taking coffee orders and holding up hemming pins wouldn't be too stressful, but damn, if I didn't come home each night drenched from a day's worth of nervous sweat.

I looked around my parents' bookshop at the tables and shelves full of glorious paperbacks with shiny covers and crisp pages, waiting to find their new homes. On the far wall, bottles of local wine and spirits sat in neat rows, arranged by taste and paired with little tags recommending an appetizer or dessert. My parents owned Spines 'n' Wines my whole life, and it was a treasure in our little English village of Berkingsley. Other small businesses lined our cobblestone sidewalks: a delectable chocolate and fudge shop, a cozy bed-and-breakfast, and a barbershop that was only open during the week, but this place here was where I spent the majority of my childhood and where the magic of daydreaming and optimism originated.

"Why are you closed so early on a Saturday this close to Christmas? And..." I swept my arm across the room, "where are all the decorations?"

No twinkling lights hung from the ceiling. The corner where our annual fir Christmas tree stood now held an artificial tree (part of my sister's and my mission to turn our parents onto the green initiative), but the usual gold tinsel and red balls were missing. It just sat there, plain and ordinary, looking like a tree plucked from the nearby woods. Now that I think about it, the door of the shop lacked its usual wreath of evergreen, and the fireplace sat bare without the springs of holly that usually adorned the top. It was less than four weeks until Christmas, and this place looked like Scrooge decided to drown his office with bottles of booze and piles of books.

"Eh, well, Alice…" Dad's hesitant response was drowned out by the shriek escaping Mum's mouth as she came at me with her arms extended and lips puckered. She planted a big kiss on my cheek and wrapped me in a warm, soft hug.

"My girl is home! A surprise visit? You little bugger. You could've rung your mum so I could have adequately planned for dinner. Will you be here all weekend? It's been, what, six weeks since we last saw you?"

"I'm home for a couple of weeks, Mum. Think of it as an early Christmas gift."

"Well, good, because you look a bit fatigued. And dear, what are you wearing? I mean, you look pleasant enough, but that's just not your typical out-and-about outfit."

I looked down at my attire. Although she was as blunt as a child's pair of scissors, she was right. My raincoat hung over my arm, showing off my comfiest jumper, which just so happened to be about ten years old and bright yellow.

Paired with my purple and black polka dot wellies, I did look a little worse for the wear.

"Yes, well, it was a long week of work, and I'm a bit knackered. Just wanted to keep comfy on the train ride in."

"Hmm." The pause in her voice told me that she didn't quite believe me, but she didn't pry. "Come on upstairs, then, and take a load off your feet. Where is your luggage? Have you rung your sister? Does Scarlett know you're visiting?"

Typical response from my mum. Not letting me get a word in. Usually, that's me, while Scarlett takes after our more reserved dad. But whenever we are in the presence of our mother, her animated spirit is the one that fills the quiet gaps and brings us back to the days when we spent hours and hours together in the small flat above the store.

"I'm actually going to stay with Emilia at her hotel." Emilia was my best friend who recently took ownership of Blackley Manor, a trendy hotel in the village. "Figured there might be a bit more space for me, and I'm eager to get caught up on some girl time." *And escape from the good cop interrogation that I was afraid to face.* "And I texted Scarlett. She's visiting Scotty's family, but she'll be back to the village soon." Scotty was her current and very serious boyfriend. *At least one of us was lucky in love.*

I began to follow Mum toward the back of the store when the tote hanging from my arm started wiggling, nudging me in the side. I tapped the fabric and gave it a quick *shush*. I had hoped to make it upstairs into the flat before ruining our cover.

Mum noticed my delay and turned to see me fidgeting. Her strawberry blonde eyebrows scrunched in puzzlement, trying to work out why I was acting like a preteen trying to sneak candy into the theater.

"What in the world is your bag doing?"

Ah, crap. I tried to stifle my giggle but failed as a cold little nub rubbed itself on my arm, and two little black beady eyes stared out at me amongst a plop of white fluff.

"Alice Marie Evans, tell me that our cat Winston just decided to give you a little extra love today, and you are not attempting a covert operation that involves some kind of four-legged creature."

Her pupils slowly expanded, and her body tensed into a fight-or-flight response. I could practically see the zones of the room mapped out in the reflection of her eyes, seeking out the nearest broom or exit.

Of course, my newest pal decided to take this moment to make the leap out of my bag. She landed on the floor like a cat (although my mum would be the first to tell you she most certainly was not one) and began a clumsy yet refined trot toward her. Probably not the best plan.

I knelt down, trying to catch her in my arms, when suddenly Winston, the store's short-haired cat, decided to make his grand entrance, leaping off the nearby book-shelf right into the path of the five-pound pile of fur. His pineapple eyes landed on his target, and a low hiss escaped his jaw, fully prepared to defend Mum's honor. While Winston was typically a lover, his loyalty belonged solely to the matriarch of our family and the four walls of the bookshop that he called home.

Yip. Yip. Yip. A little high-pitched shriek pierced the air. That little white fluff, while the most adorable problem I inherited, was also the most annoying and unpredictable solution I never thought through. Though I couldn't place the blame entirely on her. I was the prat who instantly fell in love when my last client intentionally left her alongside the discarded wardrobe after her photo shoot. I found the little pup chewing the interior liner of the luxury suitcase we were trying to market. Apparently, she was no longer fitting the image that the high-fashion model was trying to portray. However, that could have been debatable the day before when we tried to restrict the little Pomeranian from joining the company meeting.

Sheila immediately left me to deal with discarding the *minor inconvenience*, and of course, the soft-hearted idiot that I am, I took her back to my flat that night.

Yip. Yip. Yip. She barked right back in Winston's face, such a feisty, bold response to the precarious situation she found herself in.

Before a battle of the house pets could disrupt my merry homecoming, my dad stepped in and gathered Winston in his arms, stroking his gray-blue coat repeatedly. Playing fair, I scooped my teammate into my arms, lifting her beside my smiling face, trying to emphasize her impossibly cute size. Clearing my throat, I said in my most cheerful voice, "This is Pippy. Pippy, meet my mum and dad. Oh, and Winston." I rubbed my face against hers and whispered, "Don't worry. He'll warm up to you."

"What is that erratic little creature doing here?" my mother asked with frantic distaste. She had retreated to the steps and now had her arms firmly crossed over her chest, looking down at me from the second stair.

"She's not erratic. She's just a bit energetic. She's been taking a kip in my bag for the last hour. I promise you'll fall in love with her, Mum."

"Alice. I would walk through fire for you and your sister, but I'm not sure if I can get over my fear of tiny pups, even for you."

"Add that to the list of why I'm staying at Blackley Manor. I already settled it with Emilia. I just didn't want to leave Pippy there when we've only just arrived. I'm sure she would give the guests quite a surprise."

She sighed. "Well, keep her in your arms or your bag. I'm not ready to leave this life from a heart attack yet. I have Christmas dinner to prepare for."

"Yes, Mum. I solemnly swear that this little squish will remain by my side in your presence."

"Alright then, smart-arse. Follow me. I'll put a brew on for you. I've got some fresh scones and jam from Mae's Eatery, freshly prepared by William just yesterday."

William was the local baker and a dear friend of the family, not to mention somewhat of a treasured figure in our small village. Everyone knew everyone in Berkingsley. It was just the way it was. I loved knowing I had friends and confidants every which way growing up. I never thought I'd leave. But I've lived in the city of London for over a year now, and I've felt myself grow more into who I'm meant to be. Independent and kind as I've always tried to be. But, also just more comfortable with myself, quirks and all. The closer I leaned towards thirty, I guess it's to be expected. I still had a few years to go, though.

I trailed behind her up the stairs to the flat I called home and took a seat at the small round table in the kitchen, my back to the window, the spot that had been mine since I was a tot. A half-completed puzzle lay on the table in front of me.

"Oh, good Lord, Mum. Is that Harry Styles?" The image displayed on the table showed him in just a Santa hat and suspenders, the bottom half still incomplete. "Please tell me he's wearing trousers. Are you making sure all the bits and pieces are intact for Sunday night puzzle club? Yes, all puns intended." I delighted in making Mum blush, as she's usually the one who embarrasses the Evans girls in public.

"Oh, you cheeky thing! Heavens, no. This one is just for me. Kathryn is bringing the puzzle tomorrow. This week's theme is *Christmas on the Farm*."

"Ah, yes. Harry would definitely not make the cut. You'd be going for the wrong type of rooster." I flashed her a toothy smile. "Where in the world did you find this puzzle, anyway?"

"Amazon, dear. They have everything you can dream up. Now stop teasing your old lady and drink up."

I nodded, taking a sip from the cup she placed before me. Black tea with milk and a hint of sugar. Exactly the way I liked it. I wrapped my hands around it, absorbing the warmth and letting it fill my belly and dissolve my worries. A sigh floated from my lips. It felt good to be home.

"Where's Rian, darling?"

Three simple words that completely destroyed the perfect illusion I had so desperately succumbed to. I never thought I'd be that girl in her mid-twenties who shamelessly falls in love for the first time and seamlessly sees this man in every future chapter of her life. But I had with Rian. It started mostly as a playful hookup: lazy mornings in bed and afternoon picnics in the woods where we spent most of our time half-clothed, learning about each other under a blanket. But then it quickly turned into dreams of two children and a cozy house with a sunflower garden just outside the city. Now he was gone, and I was stuck like a stalled engine on the countryside, left figuring out how to fix what was broken inside and get myself back home. I was steadily finding my way, and I didn't want the disappointment or concern from my family slowing down the progress.

"He's on the RAF base this weekend. He might join next week if he can get the time off," I lied.

"Good, good. They really instill discipline in those young pilots, don't they? Working through the Christmas holiday. Let me know when he'll be joining us for a Christmas roast. I hope he's able to go home and visit his ma and sisters, too. The holiday just lacks the usual magic without your kids, even if they aren't young anymore."

Her voice held no judgment, but I internalized it and added it to the imaginary load I carried. I reached my hand across the table and placed it over hers.

"I know, Mum. I'm so grateful I'll be home for the holidays this year. Now, let's find Harry some pants," I said, reaching for a puzzle piece.

"Okay, Alexis," she ordered the music speaker. "Play Harry Styles. Your father hates my taste in music, but I tell him it keeps me young."

Something hit me then. Why were we listening to Harry Styles and not our usual Christmas playlist full of cheesy classics? I looked up at her, studying her steady expression, not giving away any hints at the change that seemed to overcome the bookstore.

"You know, Mum, I noticed the shop is missing its usual festive embellishments. Why's the tree as bare as a newborn's bottom, and when did Harry Styles replace Michael Bublé'?"

Completely ignoring me, she exclaimed, "Oh look, dear! Harry does have pants! And that's why he doesn't fit into this week's puzzle club theme. I'd better call Kathryn and make sure she's bringing the puzzle tomorrow." She got up from her seat to make the call.

The holidays, it seemed, were going to feel different this year for more than one reason.

CHAPTER TWO

'Tis the Damn Season
(and Other Taylor Break-up Songs)

"Looks like Maggie found a new best friend," Emilia proclaimed as we walked our pups along the cobblestone sidewalk in the heart of the village. Emilia took her role as step-mum to Maggie, an Australian Shepherd, very seriously after she became engaged to her fiancé, Theo, last summer. The afternoon sky was quite overcast, and frost hung on the tips of the grassy yards we passed. We were careful to avoid any icicles that hung from the thatched roofs of the familiar brick storefronts while we strolled. At least my feet were warm and cozy, nestled in my favorite wool socks.

"Indeed. Maybe even quicker than we did, although I'm glad we aren't as close as they are." My nose scrunched up as Pippy chased after Maggie, sniffing her behind as they walked. I gently tugged the leash back. "No, no, Pippy.

Boundaries are an important part of every relationship. And I'm going to say that this is definitely a boundary you shouldn't cross."

Emilia let out an easy laugh. "I'm so happy you're back in town for a few weeks. What mischief are we going to get into? My life is mundane without you in it."

We were practically inseparable before I started my hectic job. Emilia was my other half. I bounced every idea off her and shared every detail of my manic lifestyle in our daily conversations. She added that little swirl of America to my afternoon tea with a pot of coffee, and I brought the clotted cream and scones. Always the voice of reason, she helped keep me in line while I encouraged her to long jump right over it.

"Ah, yes. I know," I said, gathering my shoulder-length black hair behind my head. "I'm thinking about starting a new marketing business where I recommend touristy activities to bored Americans like yourself."

"A bit snarky today, aren't we?" Emilia asked gently, looking over at me.

"Well, I said bored, not boring. I love you too much for name-calling. But I'm sorry. I didn't mean to sound so miserable. I'm not feeling myself lately and not sure how much joviality I'm looking for."

She leaned over and gave me a side squeeze. "I know. I'm sorry if I've been annoyingly peppy. I thought I'd try to cheer you up, but I can join in your misery if that's what you need today. I just want to be sure we have more happy days than crappy ones these next few weeks. Promise me that, at least?"

I pointed to our girls, who were both squatting and doing their business behind the flowerless hydrangea bush outside the local pub.

"Not sure if we're off to a good start. Things look pretty crappy from my viewpoint."

We both looked at each other before bursting into laughter. I hooked my arm through Emilia's and put my head on her shoulder.

"Why's it hurt so bloody much? When's it going to stop?"

"I don't know, Alice. But it will. I promise. I've learned that grief takes on different forms. You're in the hardest part right now."

"But I'm tired of being here. It's almost been two months since Rian shipped off to Cyprus." Two months since he decided that we would be better off apart. Not just miles apart but living two different lives. Different homes. Different dreams. Different lovers.

"He's a shithead, and you deserve better. Should I rally the forces tonight? It's been a while since we got the gang together." The gang, meaning her fiancé, and our two friends, Noah and Trevor.

"I can't believe I'm saying this, but I'm not sure Em. I'm just not in the mood."

"Wait a minute. Alice, the five-shots-and-still-talking-straight girl, doesn't want to go out? Maybe I need to be more concerned about you than I thought. What if we start small? We'll just go to the pub." She nodded her head towards the building behind our pups. "No clubbing or trips into London. Come on, please? I can't take seeing you so sad and just...well...not yourself."

I narrowed my eyes, looking at the lines of concern etched on Emilia's forehead. "Fine. I'll do it. But not tonight. I want to just hang with you and drown my emotions in crisps and ice cream."

"I'm always down for that. Netflix is ready and loaded. But first, it's teatime, my dah-ling." She said that last bit in her god-awful British accent, the one she only brought out when she was trying to make someone laugh or cringe. I just shook my head at her.

"Still not any better? Well, damn. I've been here for a year and a half now and still can't nail it."

"Yeah, that's probably never going to happen, Em. You should probably just let that dream go."

"As long as Theo keeps calling me *love*, I guess I'll survive." She pulled her phone out and looked at the time on the screen. "But only if we get some caffeine in my veins, pronto."

As I brought the third cup of tea of the day to my lips, I took in the scene at the cafe. It was quite busy for four o'clock, and I wondered if others found the warmth from the embers crackling in the fireplace as comforting as I did. It helped ward off the dampness that accompanied the returning drizzle and made our hair soggy and frigid.

"So, are we keeping this power hour a secret from Theo?" I asked. "I kind of feel like we're breaking a friend code here, stopping at this cafe instead of Mae's Eatery." Mae's Eatery was the restaurant Theo owned and managed right in the center of our village. Modern with a farmhouse twist. It served fresh local foods and wines and also had a full espresso bar.

Emilia smirked as she put a small biscuit into Maggie's mouth. "I come here every so often to keep Theo off my scent. If I only got my free lattes from his place, I might run it out of business." She leaned back against the oversized fluffy pillow on the couch we were sitting on and crossed her legs. "I've already told you how I've desperately been trying to convince him Blackley Manor needs an espresso machine."

"Yeah, I remember. How's that proposition turning out?"

"He told me just to send the hotel guests to his restaurant. I won't admit that the machine's really for me."

Pippy started nipping at my toes, looking for another biscuit. Another perk of this café was that they allowed pups inside, even providing a big communal bowl of water near the door to wash down their free dog treats. I hadn't taken notice before, but now that I had a new four-legged rugrat to keep happy, it was a welcomed addition and only added to the cozy vibes of the place.

"One more, Pippy, and that's it." I held my hand out to her, and her little snout gobbled up the treat in a frenzy. It was amazing how a thing so miniature-sized could have an appetite the size of a giraffe.

"She's the perfect pet for you, Alice. Your personalities certainly seem to jive."

"Yes, we are both the spunky sort, aren't we Pips?" I lifted all of her five pounds of fluff to my face and rubbed my nose against hers. "Thanks again for letting me stay at the hotel, even though we're breaking the 'no pets' policy. I promise I'll make sure she doesn't wee inside."

"Just remember to take her out the back door so guests don't get suspicious. We have you in a back room next to our apartment, so it shouldn't make a difference, but I'd like to avoid any complaints from grumpy guests."

"Got it. Do not enrage the holiday grinches." I took another gulp of tea, and my thoughts started drifting away from our light chit-chat. That's how things went these days. I would be my usual chipper self for hours at a time, tucking the sad moments away in the back of my mind while I made small talk with colleagues or helped organize the fashion selections behind a new campaign at work. But then, *bam*. A song would come on the radio, or a quiet moment to myself would allow my brain to remember, and my heart would begin to ache.

My mind overflowed with anxiety as I thought about Mum and Dad. The Christmas season was one they eagerly waited for all year, as did everyone else in Berkingsley. It was a common sight to see all the businesses in the village adorned with lights and sparkles in early November. Once old Mr. Bromson, the head of the Post Office, strung lights across the front window, it was fair game for everyone to follow suit. Do it too early, and you lived in fear that your letterbox might be stuffed with old, stinky socks. He was the village authority on holiday celebrations.

By Mr. Bromson's timeline, the village most likely had become a winter wonderland weeks ago. With the whole street aglow, it was impossible for my parents to forget about hanging the icicle lights from the roofline or filling the window display with the fake, cottony snow that sat perfectly amongst the ceramic Christmas village set. Where was little George pulling the sled with the tree or Maeve ice skating with her forest critters decked in red stocking hats? These two-inch figurines were the root of many fights between my sister Scarlett and me growing up. Veiny crack lines glued together with the messy precision of a child are still visible on many of them. But not this year. The entire display was missing, along, it seems, with the Christmas spirit of the shop.

My already anxious mind churned out question after question. Was Ma or Dad ill and couldn't find the energy to decorate? Dad's eyes seemed to miss the spark they usually held when he greeted a new customer. Why was the shop closed so early during one of the busiest seasons, and what was with the boxes Dad was unloading? He usually only stocked a few books or bottles of wine at a time, choosing to unbox inventory the day he received it instead of once a week, mirroring his claim that one should never do tomorrow what one can do today. Were they upset that I hadn't visited in a while and didn't want to decorate in case I was absent for Christmas? *I just didn't know what to think.*

"And that's why I won't ever join Theo at the hardware store again. He's on his own for this next kayak-building project." Emilia paused, waving her hand in front of my face. "Earth to Alice. Are you here with me?"

A single thought suddenly seized my mind. "Emilia, are you free tomorrow?"

"Yes, actually, I am. Sundays are my day off. No piano students and no rehearsal for myself." Besides owning

Blackley Manor, Emilia was also a talented pianist who performed throughout Europe during the year. "And like I just said, Theo has taken this new woodworking hobby to the extreme and holed himself up in the back shed, building himself a kayak for when spring comes around. I love his creativity and sense of adventure, but I will never understand his eagerness to work outside for hours on end. I know that winters aren't as cold here as they are back in Boston, but still. You won't catch me building anything in this weather. Ha. Who am I kidding? I won't be building kayaks in any weather."

"Alright," I said, interrupting her, "I know exactly what will cheer me up. Let's go back to Blackley Manor and get our Christmas princess movie marathon started. I'm ready to get into the holiday spirit. I'll tell you my plan as we walk."

"Finally! You don't have to tell me twice!" She took a last sip from her mug, tucked her long blonde hair into her wool pom-pom hat, and gathered Maggie's leash. "Let's go!"

CHAPTER THREE

Rockin' Around the Christmas Tree
(in an Elf Costume)

Playing Secret Santa required three things:

❄ A fake-it-til-you-make-it love for early mornings.

❄ A tolerance of all things Christmasy, especially artificial polyester snow and garland covered in flakes of glitter that stick to freaking everything.

❄ And an assortment of elves to help you, which, in this case, a best friend would do.

The walk over to my parents' store was cold but pleasant. The early morning crisp nipped at my cheeks, and the smokey aroma of firewood burning from chimneys reminded me I was no longer in the city. While the chill had me speed-walking like the heroine in a clown-filled horror film, I felt an aura of peace settle over me. There was just something about the stillness of an early morning that restored the soul.

I arrived at the doorstep of Spines 'n' Wines a bit after six, in all my hoho glory, wearing my favorite Christmas jumper paired with thick candy cane tights and an elf hat. I woke up eager and ready to completely transform the shop into a winter wonderland before my parents ventured downstairs. I dug through my purse, looking for the spare key. *Where could it be? I know I tossed it in here.* Gently pushing the ball of fur that sat inside over a smidge, I found them warm and comfy under my pup's bottom. "Pippy, you cheeky thing. You really don't want to see Winston, do you? Well, I'm absolutely sure he feels the same."

As I nudged the wooden door open, the delicious scent of paper and ink infiltrated my senses. Sweet, like almonds and vanilla. *Ahh,* this had to be one of the most comforting smells in the world. A shop full of books. It took every ounce of self-restraint in me not to grab some novels from the front table and get lost in the pages. Mum's stern voice filled my head. "This is not a library, Alice. It's a bookstore, and we can't sell books if someone's already pawed their way through them."

That didn't always stop me, though. When I was younger and she was busy preparing meals upstairs, my dad would sometimes sneak a book to me with a wink and an unspoken agreement that I would leave the spine and pages as pristine as I received them. Once, I had forgotten and left a book open while Scarlett and I played outside.

God, I remember the panic, the over-dramatic fear that entered a child's head when she broke a cherished item of the family. I was petrified of what Ma would say and equally afraid that Dad would never loan me a book from the store again. That incident was actually what led me down the path of fashion, right into the guiding arms of my Aunt Lily, who was visiting at the time.

Aunt Lily was the epitome of a fashion-forward woman. Divorced, she lived on her own, somewhere outside of Berkingsley, somewhere big and adventurous in my childhood imagination, and she wore the most remarkable silk shirts and wool cashmere coats. She was spectacular and worldly in my ten-year-old eyes. When she found me frantically ironing the pages of the misfortunate book, she instantly took me under her wings. "Irons are not for books, dear. Here, let me show you an easier way." She brought her portable steamer over from her hotel and showed me the proper way to get wrinkles out of clothing and… well…paper. One thing led to another, and I soon found myself sorting through her luggage, trying on her headbands, necklaces, and wraps. She opened my eyes to a world outside of our village. I knew then that I wanted to dress people and make them feel as fabulous as I did while prancing around our flat in her clothes.

Back in the shop, I peeled off my coat and gloves and set my bag on the ground, freeing Pippy from her cloth prison. She instantly started doing zoomies around the room, darting between the tables of books.

"Good grief, dog. Most of the village hasn't even had their morning cuppa, and you're just bursting with the energy of a thousand Redbulls." I laughed as she ran back over to me, her tongue hanging out and her head tilted as if asking me to chase her. I tapped the top of her head with affection. "I'm sure Winston will be down soon enough, Pippy."

At the back of the shop, the storage room sat undisturbed, with the door tightly shut. I gave it a good shove (the darn thing had been sticking for years) and flicked the light switch up.

What in the bloody hell? My eyes couldn't believe the sight before me. Damn the Secret Santa plan. I frantically backed out of the room and headed toward the stairs, calling my mum's name at the top of my lungs.

"Over an inch. No, a little more. No, back just a bit. There! Perfect."

"God, Em. I hope you aren't this difficult to please in bed." I stepped back and scrutinized the stocking display we had managed to hang with a bit of tacky over the fireplace. A tad uneven, but it'll do. Now, how to keep Winston from pulling these down…

Hands on her hips, Emilia shook her head at me. "You mock me, but as I recall, you are the one who won't stop saying it needs to be perfect while humming *bippity boppity boo* nonstop."

I sunk to my knees and straightened the tree collar, taking care to rearrange the handful of fake-wrapped gifts that had shifted. "How old do you think this tree collar is?" I asked, patting down the edges that stuck up.

"Kathryn mentioned that her mother had crocheted it back when she was a tyke, so I'd have to say as old as King Charles himself." Kathryn had been the owner of the hotel before Emilia and, therefore, the previous owner of all of these crotchety decorations.

I scrunched my nose in distaste. "It's ugly as shite, but at least it doesn't smell too much like mothballs."

"Just be thankful I haven't had time to donate these old decorations yet, or we'd be stringing paper chains across the room instead." She pulled some tinsel from a box on the floor, holding it up in scrutiny. "Although, making that Christmas countdown out of red and green construction paper every season with my mom will always be one of my favorite holiday memories with her."

I looked over at Emilia and asked gently, "How are you holding up as the holidays approach without her here?"

She sighed. "This will be my third Christmas without her. Most days, I'm excited to spend the holidays with Theo as a newly engaged couple. But sometimes, I wish she was here to share in that excitement."

"That's understandable." Emilia's mother raised her alone in the suburbs of Boston, nurturing her musical abilities and supporting her as she grew into a talented pianist. They traveled together for all of her international performances until she passed away a couple of years back.

"I try to incorporate little snippets of the traditions we share as Theo and I make new ones." She smiled warmly. "Just last week, Theo and I camped out under the Christmas tree in our drawing room the night we trimmed the tree, just like I did as a kid. My mom always made extra-rich hot chocolate, from real chocolate, not the powder, and we'd load our mugs with marshmallows while we read Christmas stories in our sleeping bags. It was pure magic falling asleep to a sky full of twinkling lights."

"That sounds lovely. It's interesting to hear what others do while celebrating the season. I imagine there are some differences growing up across the pond."

"Maybe, but the sentiment is the same. I can't get over how lucky we are that I haven't gotten around to donating these decorations yet. I ordered a truckload of decorations for our first Christmas living at Blackley Manor. I just wanted it to feel like my own, you know? Especially since it's my favorite season."

"I'm surprised Kathryn allowed some of these monstrosities to hang in the hotel." I held up an old figurine of Father Christmas, who, with an indented face, looked like he should be in a Halloween display. "I mean, this is just begging to be in a Tim Burton film."

"I'm not sure she actually used any of these. Her eye for design is too strong to have allowed these in the hotel. I think some she just held on to for sentimental reasons. Now that she is living with William in his cottage, she has no room for them."

"You don't want to hang on to any of them? I mean, how can you resist the charm of this Santa Claus?" I asked, waving him in the air. "He's every child's dream. I'm putting him front and center in the display window, right next to little George and Maeve."

I set the deformed Santa in the cottony wonderland at the front of the bookshop. "I'm just so relieved this village set withstood the water damage from the pipe that burst. It's already tragic enough that the other decorations were completely waterlogged."

When I entered the storage room earlier, I hadn't seen the usual carpeted and well-organized closet that my dad prided himself in maintaining. The usual shelves of bins filled with holiday decorations, store display signs, and extra boxes of wine waiting to be stocked up front were missing. The room was stripped bare down to stone and brick, and a musty, earthy smell permeated the air.

Rushing up the stairs, calling my mum's name hysterically was probably a bit dramatic, even for me. She flew out of her room, one arm in her dressing gown, with Dad following behind in his pajamas.

"Alice? Alice, is that you?" her voice asked, dripping with worry.

Dad was a bit angrier and unforgiving once he saw me decked out as a festive elf, safe and sound, standing in the kitchen.

"What the bloody hell, Alice! What are you doing giving us a fright this early? You better have a good explanation, young lady."

"What happened to the storage room? Where are all our decorations and the extra books and supplies? Where is Fluffers and my box of journals?" Fluffers was my beloved stuffed bunny, and while I had an image to uphold in my adult life that kept him stored away, I wouldn't survive in this world if he wasn't okay.

"Oh, dear. Oh, nuts. Come and take a seat. I'll make some tea." Mum filled the kettle with water and placed it on the stovetop. To my mum, tea was always the answer to everything.

I flung my arms across my chest and sat down, no longer feeling jolly. I narrowed my eyes at my parents. "I knew you were acting weird yesterday. What haven't you told me? Spill it, you two."

My father looked at Mum, seeming to confirm what to disclose to me.

"Mm-hmm. And don't leave anything out," I added petulantly.

"Well, honey. First of all, Fluffers and your things are just fine. A few weeks ago, one of the pipes in the wall burst and completely flooded the back room. The things that weren't on the top shelves were destroyed, and of course, the room needed to be irrigated and dried out by a professional company. Luckily, very little water escaped the doorway into the shop. We just needed to replace the rug in the children's corner, and one shelf of books."

"Is that why you haven't decorated for Christmas?"

Dad looked at Mum, but her eyes quickly turned to the kettle as she poured the tea into my cup.

"Yes, Alice. We lost most of the decorations in the flood."

I could tell they were holding something back, but honestly, my brain was sorting through all the things of mine that could have potentially been lost. I wondered if my photos and yearbooks from school survived and if my early notebooks filled with fashion designs and future dreams were gone.

Back in the present, I finished arranging the final gold and red striped gift box under the tree. I took a step back to admire my work. Not half bad for what we were working with. The tree twinkled with gold lights and spirals of red ribbon cascading down from the top. White and gold bulbs hung from the branches and paired with the white buds of poinsettias, I thought it was quite pretty. Different from our usual tree adorned with tinsel and dozens of book-shaped ornaments, *but hey, change was a good thing, right?* That's what I've been telling myself these last few weeks, at least.

"I can't believe the bookstore flooded, and your parents tried to hide it from you," Emilia said, breaking up my thoughts.

"I think they are still just somewhat in shock and had hoped to get things back to normal before I came home. But I would have noticed the missing decorations, so I'm not sure what they were thinking. Who knows if they would have even told me if I hadn't barged into their flat early this morning wondering where the decorations were." I bent over and shifted through a box on the floor. "Did you say that you had a toy train we could set up in the children's area?"

"Yes, I did. Maybe it's still in Theo's truck. I'll go out and take a look." She grabbed her jacket off the stair railing and headed toward the door.

"Ah, ha. Just what we were missing," I said to myself, pulling out a string of icicle lights from the box. Grabbing the stepladder and the pile of lights, I wandered over to the romance section. I found the end and plugged it into the electrical outlet and was pleasantly surprised when the bulbs lit up in a silver radiance. "Perfect."

I stepped up on the ladder and started to drape the lights across the top shelf, highlighting books by Paige Toon, Josie Silver, and Mhairi McFarlane. The chime on the door rang as it opened, setting Pippy off in a tither. She resumed the zoomies from earlier, adding a chorus of yips as she ran.

"Pippy, please. It's just Emilia." She rushed past the nonfiction section and back around to where I stood on the ladder, reaching up and doing my best to get the strand of lights to stay on top of the shelf. *I don't think the sticky putty is going to do it. I might need to figure out another way to get these to stay.*

"Bloody dog. Knock it off." I was having a difficult time trying to get these things to stay put without her piercing bark hitting my ears, making every muscle in my body tense. Her yips grew more frantic as she circled back once again, this time knocking into the ladder. Her minuscule amount of body weight did very little to move the step, but the lights began to slide off the shelf at the same time, and as I reached to steady them, I felt myself wobble.

"Oh shite," I exclaimed, losing my balance. The lights slid off the shelf at the same time gravity took me captive, and together we fell back. *Well, if the lights weren't tangled before, they would be now.*

I prepared for my crash landing on the wooden floor, but instead felt myself sink into a broad chest and two strong arms that instantly engulfed my 5 '4 frame. I turned my head and looked up into the eyes of someone who was definitely not Emilia.

CHAPTER FOUR

Do You Hear What I Hear
(Village Gossip from the ladies)

I stared into those dark chocolate eyes far longer than the situation warranted, my mouth agape in what I'm sure was an unattractive look of befuddlement. But in my defense, the arms that caught me held on a few seconds longer than was necessary before setting me back upright on my own two feet. Even with his wool overcoat on, I could still feel the muscles in this stranger's arms when he caught me.

"Uh, nice catch." I casually swiped the hair from my face, trying to play it cool in front of this six-foot hunk of a man who looked exactly freaking like the Duke of Hastings from *Bridgerton*. This was a tad difficult while dressed like Santa's little helper, but I tried to muster all the sexy confidence built up from years of adult Halloween parties. I jut my left hip out, placing my hand on the opposite side, hoping it looked like I fully intended to fall deep into this stranger's arms.

And…he just stood there, both hands in his pocket, staring at me with humor in his eyes and a tight smile on his lips. Not saying anything. Not. One. Single. Word. Even Pippy was stunned by his standoffish demeanor, quietly sitting next to me, tilting her head in confusion at the man before her.

I cleared my throat, trying another approach. In my best customer service voice, I chirped, "Welcome to Spines 'n' Wines. Can I help you find anything?" The silence seemed to linger in the air just long enough to irritate me. Seriously, what was with this guy? Arsehole. Finally, he spoke:

"My apologies. I hadn't realized there was a children's Christmas event going on today. Are you open to the public, or shall I find my way out?" His thumb pointed back toward the exit, eyebrows raised, looking me over from my elf hat to my fuzzy slippers.

"Yes, we are. Just opened ten minutes ago, in fact, and there is no children's event. Just little me trying to make this place a little merrier and bright for the arseho…, uh, grinches who might wander in."

He grunted in reply as he turned toward a table to the right, picked up a book, and began flipping through the pages before turning it over to glance at the back cover. He had to be feigning interest because I knew for a fact that the book was a guide for menopausal women. His stoic demeanor might have passed as PMS, but his body was all testosterone.

"Going through some life changes, then?" I asked

pleasantly, managing to hide the jest in my voice. Two can play at this game.

He flipped the book to the front, taking note of the cover. He responded by lifting the book above his head, giving it a slight shake. "Ah, looking for a Christmas gift for my mum, but I don't think this one will do."

"Yeah, that will most likely get you on the naughty list this year. What are her interests? Cooking, baking, animals? The rules of social etiquette, perhaps? We also have games and puzzles in the far back corner of the store. I know my mum fancies those."

He nodded his head in response. "I'll go take a look." He started towards the far wall but hesitated for a moment. Turning back toward me, he said simply, "Thank you."

"No problem." My eyes lingered a bit too long on him as he walked away. Too bad his bland personality didn't match that perfect physique. Santa could only do so much to make wishes come true.

I returned my attention to the original problem of getting these Christmas lights secured up on the displays. It really shouldn't be so difficult. I've decorated and rearranged my flat so many times that my friends sometimes wondered if a new tenant moved in. After untangling the strands of bulbs, I climbed back up on the step ladder, carefully leaned over, and hooked the lights around an old nail I found at the top of the shelf. *Bingo.* Now, if I could just get the end of the strings to stay put…

Clunk. The lights once again rolled forward off the shelf, colliding with the wooden floor. This time, thankfully, I didn't join them in the fall. I hopped off the ladder in frustration and sank down on my hands and knees, gathering the bundle of lights. "Merry freaking Christmas," I huffed under my breath as I once again worked to untangle the strands. When I finally had them bunched in my arms, I looked up and found my view obstructed by the crotch of the one and only bookstore Duke.

"Oh, hi. May I help you?" I asked his pelvis.

Finally, a genuine smile crossed his face. His gorgeous eyes lost a bit of their intensity, replaced with humor and maybe even a bit of concern.

"I came over to ask you the same thing." He reached his hand out, and I placed mine in it, his grip tightening around my palm, pulling me to my feet. His other hand easily held a basket filled with four bottles of wine and barrel-aged whiskey. Interesting choice of reading.

"I prefer the red," I said, nodding towards his basket.

"Ah, yes. Agreed. These are for my mum and sisters. They love a dry white wine. The whiskey- that's for me. Holidays at home tend to be better with a, um, little refreshment. So, do you want me?"

"Excuse me?" I gulped, fully aware of how close our bodies stood. I probably shouldn't be able to smell the damp fabric of his jacket or the faint peppermint on his breath. Or see the veins in his forearm peeking out from the jacket sleeve. Do I want him? Well, he certainly got straight to the point, didn't he—?

"The lights." His voice pushed those sugarplum visions straight out of my head and back into the reality of Santa's bookshop wonderland. "Do you want me to help you with the lights?" he clarified.

"Um, yeah. Okay. Thank you." I pointed toward the end of the romance section. "I'm trying to hang them along this shelf. Add a little sparkle to this side of the room." I climbed the stepladder, hopefully for the last time, stringing them once again along the top, fully aware that my arse was in direct eyesight of my new personal assistant. He didn't seem to notice, though. His focus was solely on tucking the end of the lights securely behind a Christmas bear Emilia had brought over. One I had already affectionately named Mrs. Claws.

I stepped back to scrutinize our work, and the Duke followed. "Not too shabby, right?"

He nodded in agreement, his face void of any emotion.

"Right. Well, thanks for your help. I'm Alice, by the way." I propelled my hand out, and surprisingly, he didn't leave me hanging.

"Freddie. And it's quite alright. No problem at all. Could you ring me up at the till?"

"Of course. Follow me." We headed to the counter up front, Pippy close on my heels. Freddie placed the bottles of wine and whiskey on the counter, pulling his wallet out from the back pocket of his trousers.

"So, no books today, then?"

He shook his head. "You know, I don't actually know what my mum likes to read. Figured I'd browse her book-shelves and come back to pick something out."

"Is it for Christmas?" I asked, totaling his purchase and placing the bottles in a paper bag.

"Yeah, it is."

"You have a bit more time to sort it out. Tell you what. Come back and tell me what she likes, and I'll help pick out a few titles for you. This is my parents' shop. I don't live here anymore, but I'll be around the next few weeks helping out." I slid the bag across the counter toward him.

"Thank you, Alice. I'd appreciate that." His brooding eyes focused in on mine, and I felt all words momentarily escape my brain. Nodding my head, I managed to give an awkward wave goodbye as he turned and left the shop, holding the door for Emilia, who was carrying a clear bin filled with train tracks. I heard her thank Freddie as she passed by.

"Sorry it took me so long. Carol caught me outside and wanted to chat about the winter festival coming up next weekend…"

"Oh, yeah?" I asked, trying to collect my thoughts, which suddenly seemed to be darting all over the place like Pippy hyped up on one of the homemade pup biscuits I sometimes baked for her.

"It sounds like it will be a great event. She's looking for more vendors and participation from local businesses. I told her I'd gather some music students to play carols and would mention it to your parents as well. Maybe they could set up a book stand."

"Sounds like a delight. I'll let my mum know. Let's get this train set up, shall we? I'm hoping to be done and out of here before puzzle club starts, and I get plastered with questions about my love life."

"Ah, smart. How long until puzzle club?"

"About an hour. Mum said it starts at 11 a.m."

"We should have plenty of time, then." Emilia set the bin down in the children's section next to the tree. "Let's get to work!"

We did not have plenty of time. It turned out that when you were retired and eager to hear any bits of gossip that might be new in town, there was no such thing as arriving too early. One by one, the ladies from the Berkingsley Puzzle Club trickled in, faces caked in full makeup and all carrying some sort of sweet treat or savory snack.

First was Penny, the former nanny to many families around town. She gave a soft smile and a demure hello, a crumb cake in hand. She actually wasn't one to gossip, but she lived alone since her husband had recently passed, and good company was what she sought. Emilia and I engaged in polite chit-chat until Kathryn arrived next, bringing an assortment of scones and pastries from William's kitchen. Though tiny in stature, she always carried herself with the posture of a queen, and her wardrobe reflected that, too. She removed her coat, and underneath, she wore a black turtleneck sweater with a gold linen shawl covering her petite shoulders.

"Oh, so nice to see you, Alice, dear. Emilia told me you'd be home on holiday for the season. What a wonderful gift for your parents. How is your big fancy job in the city going?"

"They're keeping me busy, and I love putting my skills to work. And might I say, you look beautiful today. What a stunning wrap you are wearing! I always know who to get my fashion tips from." I winked at her. "Here, let me take those goodies, and I'll lay them out for you."

"Oh, not necessary, dear. We have our own little system here." She pulled a maroon cotton tablecloth covered in snowflakes of various sizes from her purse as the door chime rang behind us. "But you can keep laying on the compliments. An old lady like me never gets tired of hearing them."

"Well, I could go on all day–" but before I could begin, the bell on the door jangled, and a cackle of gibbering voices pulled everyone's attention away.

I muttered a few words of exasperation as I turned to greet the chatty women at the door. June and Bernice. The two queens of town gossip. It was always a fine line between wanting to hide from their game of twenty-one questions and embracing their bustling personalities. They lived at the retirement home on the outskirts of the village but always managed to know the workings of every business and resident of Berkingsley. They were a lot, but I loved them.

Bernice entered the shop first, a bonnet tied under her chin and her focus already on me. "Alice, lovely Alice. I am so happy to see you're back in town."

June shuffled in behind, unwrapping her scarf as she entered. "I already told you she was back, Bernice. I heard it from Carol."

"Well, one never knows where Carol gets her intel, June. Just last month, she mistakenly informed us that the mitten drive was extended, and we purchased all that yarn and completely missed the deadline. Now we have bins of yarn collecting dust and half-finished mittens that we need to get onto the hands of children." She hung her tan overcoat and hat on the coat rack beside the door.

"I took care of it. Theo is collecting them when we're finished and will drop them off at the children's center in Maydom. It will all get sorted out," June replied.

"What a splendid fellow that Theo is. Smart thinking, keeping him out of trouble so he doesn't go on any winter wilderness expeditions. That boy is always looking for a way to make our hearts wreck with worry." Bernice set a ceramic bowl filled with a delicious-smelling dip on the table, followed by a small container of crackers as she chatted, saying her hellos to Kathryn and Penny.

I looked over at Emilia, who was hidden from view behind a bookshelf. She was trying her hardest to hold back a laugh as they discussed her fiancé, not wanting to reveal her presence too quickly.

"Oh, I wouldn't fret too much over Theo. Emilia, here, is keeping him in line, making sure his adventures aren't too adventury." She threw me a look of disdain before poking her head out from behind the books and giving a wave.

"She's got that right. Hi, Bernice. Hi, June. So good to see you here," she said.

"We wouldn't miss Puzzle Club. It's our favorite part of the month. Wait until you see the puzzle we brought today," Bernice said, a twinkle in her eye.

Kathryn paused from smoothing the wrinkles out of the tablecloth, an annoyed look on her face.

"It's my month to bring the puzzle." She held up a box with the photo of a vintage farm truck with a tree tied to the bed, shaking it for emphasis. "It's the MacKenzie-Childs special. I made a special trip to Harrods just for the occasion."

"Oh, Kathryn. That is so lovely. A trip out to London just for the puzzle? How thoughtful," Penny said while pouring herself a cuppa from the kettle on the table.

"Oh yes, Kathryn. So very nice," June added. "It is a bit…" she wrinkled her nose, "conventional, don't you think? Bernice and I got a jolly kick out of this one. Show 'em, Bernie."

Digging into her bag, she lifted out a large box covered in more than a dozen cat faces, each making a distinct face and wearing a different outfit. One with a Santa hat, one wrapped in a present, one wearing earmuffs.

Penny laughed. "Oh, look, Alice. One even looks like you." I hoped she was referring to the elf costume and not my eyeliner. Either way, the puzzle was adorable, but I could sense trouble brewing as Kathryn's shoulders tensed and her lips puckered into a grimace. Emilia and I exchanged conspiring looks. The only catfight I wanted to witness was over who would place the last puzzle piece.

"Ladies, these are both quite festive choices. I think you should do both," I smoothly interjected, hoping to ease the tension growing in the room like a hot-air balloon.

"Yes," Emilia chimed in. "And we could glue them and frame them to hang on the wall after. Alice and I were just discussing what else this place needs to feel a bit more Christmasy."

I looked at Kathryn, who was avoiding everyone's gaze by picking up pretend crumbs from the table that was now laden with dishes, and then over to Bernice and June, who seemed to be contemplating our suggestion.

Kathryn raised her head, lifting her chin in the air. "I suppose that will work. But I am working on the vintage puzzle. It was my month to choose, after all, and cats don't even fit with this month's theme."

"You'll never find a farm without a cat wandering its grounds. But I, too, love the idea of framing them both. We could even make it a contest and have the customers vote on which they like better," Bernice said. June nodded her head in agreement.

A fresh voice joined the discussion. "No competitions, ladies. The bookstore is a place of unity, not the sort of place to get people miffed." Mum had descended the stairs, carrying a tray with wine glasses and a steaming pot that emitted scents of cinnamon and cloves. "Have a glass of mulled wine and relax. I say we do both puzzles together and make it an afternoon. Ollie can take care of the till."

"Always the wise one, Joyce," Bernice said to my mother, plucking glasses off the tray and putting one at each seat around the wooden table. "Now, to choose which puzzle we should do first…"

Oh, for cripes sake. These ladies. Mum quickly mumbled an excuse and ran back up the stairs, and I followed suit and motioned for Emilia to help me arrange the ornaments on the tree in the back of the store.

"These ladies are too much," Emilia whispered, trying to hold back a giggle.

"Tell me about it. I'm sure they'll move on to town gossip soon."

"Yeah, or begin a town feud. Time will tell." She moved a few gold ornaments to the side of the tree and retied a few poinsettia buds to the branches. "I think we did a grand job on this tree. It's gorgeous."

It was quite a beauty. I already felt my Christmas cheer meter rising to HoHoHo level, taking in the sight of the tree, front display, and lights hanging from the ceiling. Secret Santa Mission was a success.

But then, June's voice interrupted my thoughts, ruining all progress of a happy Christmas. "It's such a shame that this will be the last Christmas the bookstore will be open. It feels like more than just a part of the village. It's a part of who we all are."

My smile froze on my face. As I edged closer to the group, still hidden by a bookshelf, I heard Penny say, "I'm so glad the girls decided to decorate the place. Joyce said that Ollie has been in such a depressed state since the flood. Hasn't even given a thought to Christmas."

"Poor man. It doesn't help that most of their decorations were destroyed. And with the enormous cost of repair of the pipes and walls, well, I'm sure they didn't want to put money towards something so frivolous as decor when they can't even afford to keep the place running," Bernice said.

"Spreading Christmas cheer isn't frivolous, Bernie," June countered.

Kathryn cleared her voice. "Either way, darlings, it isn't proper to be discussing other people's finances. Especially those of our friends."

"Quite right, Kathryn." June nodded. "Thank you for that reminder. Now, let's get started on this puzzle. I just know this Meowy Catmas puzzle is going to look purrfect on the wall." They all laughed and surprisingly, not a single peep of disagreement was made.

The sounds of their joy deepened the pit that grew in my stomach. The bookstore, closing? Images of a happy Christmas suddenly transformed into a snowy mirage.

CHAPTER FIVE
I'll Be Home for Christmas
(so let's Grab a Pint)

"I'll take one more of those," I said, grabbing a pint off the bar and stealing it right from under Theo's nose. "Emilia won't mind waiting." I immediately put the glass to my mouth and swallowed a few unladylike gulps.

"I won't mind waiting for what?" she asked, suddenly appearing by my side like Houdini, back from the loo. She wrapped her arms around Theo's waist, placing her chin on his shoulder. These two were like the sickly-sweet couples you fawned over in Hallmark movies.

His lips landed on her cheek, giving her a kiss. Theo had that sexy, yet sweet boy-next-door look going on: dark brown hair that casually flopped in his baby-blue eyes and a day's worth of stubble on his face. "Hey, love. I'm glad you're back. I'm having a hard time keeping this one under control. She's already confiscated both your drinks, and I'm wondering what will happen when the order of nachos arrives."

"Hush, you," I said. "Emilia is a very generous soul. She doesn't mind helping her best friend work through her problems with a bit of alcohol and some crisps. Plus, the next round's on me."

"Okay, but let's just slow it down a bit before you get properly smashed and make some poor decisions."

I leaned over the bar and shouted an order for another round of drinks and, what the hell, another order of nachos, just to keep Theo quiet. Crikey, he was a buzzkill. As a childhood friend, he took his role of overprotective big "brother" of the Evans girls a little too far for someone who was the baby of his family. Usually, I don't mind the attention, but tonight was not the night.

We carried the collection of drinks back to our table, which sat nestled in the corner of the familiar pub. O'Riley's Place was your typical corner bar found in your typical small English village. Wooden floor, wooden walls, wooden stools that hurt my boney arse. Lingering smells of spilled beer clung to the crevices on the floor, and the greasy odor of comfort food filled the air. Seeing how it was only Monday, the place brimmed with mostly young locals from town and only two gray-haired men sitting at the counter nursing their drinks and watching the game on the telly.

"Alice, here are your nachos. Just the way you like 'em." A tall ginger placed the platter of crisps on the table, loaded with sausage and dripping cheddar cheese and topped with a fried egg.

"Thanks, Ben." I flashed my former school chum a smile.

Extra jalapeños. There were perks to drinking in your hometown. Gosh, my head was swarming between feelings of nostalgia from being back home to waves of nausea from worrying over my parents' situation. Not to mention, I was also trying to fill that empty void of loneliness that existed without Rian by my side. *Seriously, who breaks up three months before Christmas?* That's barely enough time to turn a rebound hookup into a proper relationship before the downtown shops begin blaring Christmas love songs through their outdoor speakers. And, while I'm grateful for my parents, a little wrapped box from my mum sitting under the tree just doesn't bring the same kind of holly jolly feelings. Socks. She always got me socks. Last year, they had sheep on them. The year before, donuts with smiley faces on them. Yeah, socks just didn't carry the same sentiment as a little blue Tiffany's box sitting under the tree.

"Alice, you'd better get eating before we demolish these babies," my friend Trevor nudged, his considerate spirit always shining through. He and his partner, Noah, received the emergency text message from Emilia saying that we needed the group together tonight, and they made sure to catch the rush hour train from London, where they both lived and worked. Trevor was the Assistant Supervising Intendent of Talent at The Royal Albert Music Hall, where he met Emilia last year during her piano tour. This meant that he hired the musicians and made sure everything ran smoothly while they were visiting and performing in the London theater. Noah sold properties around the city and nearby countryside. "And seriously, Noah, easy on the beans, or you'll be on the sofa tonight."

"Well, maybe tonight is the perfect night to head to Em and Theo's for a viewing of that movie."

"What movie?" I asked, stuffing a crisp smothered with queso into my mouth, making sure at least two jalapeños topped the bite.

"Show Alice the photo," Trevor prompted, nudging Noah in the side. He obligingly swiped the screen on his mobile and held it up to my face, showing a photo of an adorable brown and white furry creature wearing a Santa hat.

"Aww, well, isn't that the cutest little guy? He and Pips could be playmates. What is it?"

"Just wait a minute, Alice. You're never going to believe it." Trevor said, his eyes animated with mischief.

"Oh, God," Theo leaned his forehead into Emilia's shoulder, rubbing it side to side in jest. Emilia just giggled.

"What, guys? Come on. I don't get it." My bottom lip pursed out in a sullen pout. I hated being left out of an inside joke. It felt as if I had been abandoned at a rest stop after running in to buy snacks for a cross-country road trip.

"This." Noah shoved the phone back in my face. But this time, the image was far from the adorable little scruff he had shown me a minute ago. Sure, it donned a Santa hat, but it was more like an evil elf that you'd find overseeing the naughty list.

"Blimey, what in the ever frickin' hell is that?" A lizard-like creature with giant ears and teeth dripping with slimy drool stared back at me. The origin of many childhood nightmares, I'm sure. I pushed his hand away, eager to erase the image from my mind.

"According to Emilia, that is a character from a holiday classic back in the States," Noah said, tucking his phone securely back in his trouser pocket.

"Americans have a sick way of celebrating the birth of Jesus. Geez, Em," I replied. I looked over at her with my judgy eyes.

"Come on, guys. It was a classic in the '80s before I was born. My mom and I would watch it every Christmas. Those little guys have a special place in my heart." She looked adoringly at Theo. "Plus, I don't know how you have never heard of them. Theo has!"

"Yeah, but I never saw the movie before I met you. It's all well and good, love, until they get wet or fed after midnight. Then it's all creepy, drooling monsters wreaking havoc on Christmas. It's called *Gremlins,* and apparently, there are two movies, although Milia has only forced me to watch the first." Theo leaned toward Emilia and pulled her closer. "I told her that if we're going to watch another Christmas movie with puppets, then *The Muppet Christmas Carol* is as far as I'll go."

Noah grew excited. "Oh, mate, that's a good one. Michael Caine is a legend and how can anyone dislike Kermit the Frog? My vote for movie night is that one."

"Yes, please. I absolutely dig a movie with singing. Count me in! Alice, what do you think?" Trevor leaned in, eager to hear my response.

"Hmm?" My mind had wandered from the juvenile problems of movie night back to the news of my parents losing their shop. I had to do something about it. I was never one to admit defeat; I always found a way to make things happen.

That's what made me so good at my fashion marketing job. I learned to style the actors and models in a way that attracted attention to the products and ads, yet appeased the usually rigid opinions of the higher-ups that walked into our office. It was a magical gift I somehow came to possess over the years. But even though I secured my dream job, I had just started in the position last summer and was making meager wages. And without Rian's contribution toward rent, I could barely afford my London flat. I didn't have enough money to help my parents with this problem.

"Truthfully, I have bigger problems on my mind. Do any of you have an idea on how to raise a significant sum of money in a short amount of time?"

The group fell quiet, suddenly interested in what scheme I was proposing. "How short are we talking, Alice, and how much?" Theo inquired. He looked over at Emilia inquisitively and with concern. She just stared at me, the synapses firing behind her eyes practically visible from where I sat. It was clear she had given it some thought since our conversation yesterday.

"Thousands. And pretty much by last month."

Trevor's eyebrows came together in confusion, Noah's eyes grew wide in disbelief, and Theo raised his fist to his mouth in thought. The air sat laden with the defensive response of testosterone. "Is everything okay, Alice?" A slight pause sat between each word.

Emilia cut through the tension at the table with her peppy American accent. "Guys, guys. Relax. She's fine. Put your knives back in your pockets."

I ran my hand down my ponytail, which sat low in the back, trying to appear casual enough to calm their thoughts. "Yeah, no coppers after me, boys. But I'm looking for somewhat of a Christmas miracle. Do you think you can help me?"

My eyes scanned the faces at the table, all attentive and full of worry. I hoped with all my heart that they could.

Everyone loves a winter festival. My brain was in overdrive with all the ideas bouncing around. My friends hadn't let me down with their practical imaginations, and for once, I felt hopeful that we could get my parents through this financial hump.

The cold air hit us like a brick wall as we walked through the pub door and out into the winter night. I felt better now that we had a plan in place. Maybe this Christmas wouldn't be so bad. I could play Secret Santa for real and give my parents the best gift yet. This wasn't the end of Spines 'n' Wines. I just knew it. Sure, the only thing keeping me warm at night was a small heap of fur, but I survived the many months that Rian was away during boot camp last year. I could certainly survive without him now. Which reminded me—

"Oh, shite, I left my takeaway at the table. Pippy will be cranky if I don't bring her my leftovers. I'll be right back."

"She's a dog. I'm pretty sure she won't even realize it, kid," Theo said, his arm linked through Emilia's.

"Oh, you don't know how spoiled she is. Just wait until you meet her. She thinks she's royalty."

"Want me to go back with you?" Emilia asked, lifting her head from Theo's shoulder.

"No, I'll just be a second. You two can warm the truck up, and I'll be back in a jiffy."

I gave a quick hug goodbye to Trevor and Noah before turning around and heading back to the far end of the pub. I reached our table and exhaled a sigh of relief, glad that the server hadn't cleaned up yet. "I got you, Pips," I murmured, thinking about how excited she would be over the leftover beef kabobs long gone cold.

"See ya, Ben." I waved goodbye to my old friend at the bar as I walked past, the Christmas spirit beginning to flow through my veins now that I had other people sharing the stress that weighed me down. This little village was built on community, and the connections families had were forever weaved together like an old knitted blanket. Neighbors showed up. They took care of each other. Especially if it involved an event that included food, gossip, or entertainment. Even a casual friendship like the one Ben and I had formed years before in school still held merit in Berkingsley. You really couldn't escape it.

"Later, Alice. Stay warm," Ben replied, stopping the flow of ale from the tap he controlled. He slid the glass over to a figure sitting solo at the bar wearing a forest green sweater that stretched tightly across the muscles in his back. I stared for a second too long and then laughed at myself. Even the sight of a man's back intrigued me these days. I needed some serious distraction to get me through this holiday season without a beau. At least the bookshop's problems provided that and more.

"Oh, it's Santa's jolly elf again," the figure mumbled playfully before lifting the glass to his mouth.

My eyebrows scrunched in puzzlement as I looked down at my outfit, which, besides the red plaid kitten heels, in no way resembled anything festive. My outfits were often an extension of my feelings, and tonight, I had tried to extinguish my anxiety over the bad karma involved in losing my childhood home and future husband in the same year. Hadn't worked, of course. So, what did this guy mean by Santa's jolly elf?

"Excuse me, sir? I didn't quite catch that."

He arched his head my way. "Just noticed that you are far from Santa's workshop tonight."

His face came into full view despite the shadows from the bar's poor lighting edging in like ink stains across his cheeks. Those coffee drop eyes. That strong jawline. The elf comment suddenly made complete sense.

I twirled my hair with my fingers, batting my eyelashes dramatically. "Santa only needs me on the weekends. I have other responsibilities during the week. Looks like you do, too."

He nodded, the corners of his lips slightly upturned, motioning to the stool next to him. "Care to join me, Alice?"

The casual shrug of my shoulders hid my keen awareness that he remembered my name. Sorry, Pippy. Suddenly Mummy's got her own midnight snack.

"Sure, I could use one more drink. Let me just text my friend to let her know."

ME: Ran into the Duke from the bookshop. Gonna stay for another drink.

EMILIA: Okay. Want me to send Theo back for you in a while?

ME: Nah. I'll call an Uber.

EMILIA: At this time? There might not be any. You're not in London anymore.

ME: I'm the one who grew up here, remember Miss Boston? I'll be okay.

EMILIA: Alright. Have fun. Be safe.

ME: XO

I pulled up the rideshare app and booked a ride for an hour from now. Nothing to it.

"Everything okay?" Freddie asked, nodding his head at my fingers tap dancing on my mobile.

"Yep." The air sat still in the silence that followed, but surprisingly, any awkwardness that tended to accompany it was comfortably absent. We were just two people in a bar, having a drink, deep in our own thoughts, but somehow on the same wavelength. Well, to be honest, my thoughts were racing at full speed through my head. This guy was such a hunk, but he was also such a mystery. He was aloof but somehow still friendly. I didn't quite understand his game. I had never met a man like that.

"What can I get you to drink?" he asked at the same time I called out, "Ben, can I get an Irish Coffee?" His voice was smooth and even, like melted chocolate cascading over the sides of a fondue fountain.

Across the bar, Ben lifted his chin in acknowledgment and a knowing smile. Maybe he knew what was going on here, but I sure as hell didn't. It had been one of those monochromatic days where I accomplished nothing much beyond laundry, answering work emails, and walking Pippy, but the mental load I carried left every inch of my body exhausted. The moment Freddie turned his head from the bar, though, I knew I wasn't going anywhere. His aura enclosed me like a warm fire I couldn't ignore.

"So, um, Fff—" I paused, feigning memory loss. Like his presence at the bookshop the day before hadn't triggered an hour of girl talk between Emilia and me. But he didn't have to know that.

"Freddie," he replied, unbothered.

"So, Freddie, what's your story? What are you doing alone in a pub in Berkingsley on a Monday night? It's not exactly the type of place you visit expecting to bring someone home without being the talk of the village the next day."

He leaned toward me, breathing in my ear, "I hadn't realized you expected to come home with me. A bit quick for my tastes, but if you insist…"

My mouth hung open at his insinuation, and as I prepared to give him a piece of my mind, the left side of his mouth turned up into a delicious, goofy grin.

"I'm sorry. That was a lame joke. I would kill any bloke who even remotely thought those things about my sisters. Can I start again? I promise I have better pickup lines."

I nodded hesitantly but couldn't hold back my smile. "It's alright. I'm not that easily offended. Go on. Tell me why you're here, then. I'm all ears."

"Believe it or not, I wasn't supposed to be that lonely bloke at the bar. I had plans with my sisters, but Sophie, the oldest, is scrubbing vomit out of my nephew's carpet, Nella forgot that the newest season of *The Bachelor* starts tonight, and my baby sister, Lulu, decided a night out with her big brother wasn't as cool as a last-minute date with her boyfriend." He shrugged nonchalantly. "So, here I am."

"Wait," I exclaimed in shock. "Shite, *The Bachelor* starts tonight? That totally slipped my mind. I'm off, too." I began to shift my weight off the bar stool when I felt the light pressure of his hand on my shoulder.

"Really?" His caramel-laced voice suddenly lacked its easy coolness, sounding more like an eleven-year-old boy who was turned down by a girl on the playground, and I almost felt bad for pretending to be the fourth female tonight who had better plans than hanging with him.

I settled back in my place. "Nah, I'm just playing with you. I have too much drama in my own life. I don't need to watch the telly to get my fill."

He seemed to settle back comfortably on his stool. "Want to talk about it? Or just drink about it?"

I thought for a minute. Did I want to talk about it? I usually word-vomited all my problems to anyone who would listen. But I was tired of feeling heartbreak. Tired of replaying the reel of my non-existent future with Rian through my head. I had successfully removed him from the physical parts of my life, having redecorated the flat we shared and converting it back to the living space of a single occupant. I trashed the chipped mug he used every single morning for the only dose of caffeine he allowed himself a day. *I should have seen the signs then. Who has that kind of self-restraint? Only a psychopath, that's who.* I added an elaborate shoe rack on the side of the closet where his combat clothing and service uniform had neatly hung in rows organized by length. His shelf in the living room, usually lined with plastic cases of shooter video games, now held a framed photo of me and Pippy, as well as a treat jar that said, "It's treat o'clock somewhere!" But even though I removed these everyday reminders of Rian, his smell still lingered on the right side of the bed, and his promises of forever still echoed throughout my head when I walked Pippy in the early mornings.

"No. I think I'm okay," I lied.

"Okay." He turned his head toward the telly that was hanging adjacent to the rows of glasses elevated on a wooden shelf near the ceiling. A football game played on the screen with captions running across the bottom.

"You like football? I pegged you as more the literary type."

"A guy can't like sports and reading? Where did you pick up that stereotype?"

"I guess my personal experience has been very limited-" I cleared my voice, "-in that area. Date nights in my last relationship always revolved around what time the gym was open and whether there was another level to beat in his video game.

He grunted. "Sounds like you've been with boys, not men."

"Yeah, I guess you could say that." I took a long drink from my mug. Eager to change the topic, I asked, "What's your favorite book, then?"

On the screen, one of the players made a goal, and reactively, Freddie's fist slammed against the counter, and a jumble of obscenities flew out of his mouth.

"Come on, mates," he growled. "You have one freakin' job." His hands hung in the air, pleading with the universe over a silly game. I cautiously looked over at him, wondering how this was going to go. Is this the moment his attractiveness took a dive with the appearance of an angry temper?

To my surprise, his body calmly rotated in my direction, a sort of Jekyll and Hyde act, saying, "I love a good saga. *Lord of the Rings* or the Ken Follet series. Something that keeps me invested in the story and takes me to a new place. I quite enjoy history, actually. I studied the Medieval period at King's College a few years back."

"History? Blech. I mean, I love a good fictional saga, but you wouldn't catch me reading one of those dry textbooks even if it held the key to the fountain of youth."

"Well, actually, you can find the answer to eternal youth there. Have you ever heard of the Spanish explorer Juan Ponce de Leon?"

"Nope, nope, and nope. I refuse to listen to a history lesson when I have enough problems in the present to worry about. Sorry, Professor Freddie, I won't be pouncing on any Juan Leons tonight."

A chuckle erupted compulsively from his gorgeous face despite his best intentions to maintain a serious disposition.

"Careful there, Champ. You've got a bit of, um, something on your face." I motioned with my thumb to the side of my face, trying to show him where.

He brushed his hand across his chin but came up empty.

"To the left. No, a bit more. Nope, too far. Oh, just let me." I leaned over, totally evading his personal space and inhaling a faint undertone of pine and cypress. The pads of my fingers brushed against his trimmed stubble, and the intimacy of my action suddenly felt enormous. I paused for a beat, unsure what my next move should be. The easy companionship I felt around him in the last hour changed as abruptly as my daily wardrobe.

Oxygen finally found its way back to my head, and I returned to my stool, my cheeks aflame like the fireplace behind us. Electricity. That's what I felt when I touched his face. A jolt that shocked my heart, twisted my stomach, and finally settled in my lady bits. Oh, shite. I had the hots for this guy.

Curiously, he seemed to be immune to my agitation and simply replied, "Thanks."

We chatted on and off for the next twenty minutes, sharing trivial facts, like what our favorite trilogy was and if we were more productive during the mornings or at night. Nothing too deep or personal. Just a relaxing conversation far from any of the stressful triggers in my life. The more we talked, the more Freddie warmed up. We had just gotten into a debate over what was the superior snack in the cheese world, cheese fries or nachos, when my mobile buzzed from where it sat on the bar. The driver, who was set to pick me up in ten minutes, which, by the way, was the time the bar was closing, had canceled. Perfect. It was almost eleven, and I really didn't want to bother Emilia and Theo when they most likely had just crawled into bed.

"Something wrong?" Freddie must have noticed my annoyance. I wonder what gave it away: the unseemly words I had huffed at my phone or my pissed-off body language.

"My ride just canceled." I hesitated for a second. *Should I ask Freddie for a ride home?* I didn't even know his last name, but heck, I hadn't even known my driver's first name, although that would be changing once I rated his sorry arse for ghosting me.

Let's see. I mentally checked off what I knew about this guy. *He has a mum and three sisters. He's into sports and reading and has a weird interest in history, which does give off a bit of a nerd vibe, but eh, he's super hot, so that pretty much negates his peculiar choice in studies. Plus, do I have any other alternative?*

"Any chance you can give me a ride home?"

"Yeah, sure. But I walked here. I'm staying at the B & B just a block away. My car's parked there. I could give you a ride from there if that works."

"Yes! That would be great. Thank you. I can't believe this. I've never had a driver cancel on me. What ridiculously bad luck."

"Well, we are in Berkingsley, Alice. A bit different from catching a ride in London."

"How did you know I live in the city?"

"Wild guess." He smirked. "Come on, ma 'lady. I shall escort you to your ride home."

He offered his forearm for support as I hopped off the stool, and I coyly leaned into him. We grabbed our jackets off the coat rack and bundled up for the winter night. A steady drum of cold rain greeted us as we stepped outside. I looked down at my footwear.

"Guess I should have worn my elf shoes," I said to Freddie with a frown.

"That's how I knew you weren't from around here. No one who lives in Berkingsley chooses style over comfort. Hop on my back."

"What? Nuh-uh. No way."

"Alice, be practical. It's only a block away. It's either that or get sloshing wet."

My lips twisted in deliberation. I loved these heels, and I'd admit they cost me a small fortune, but I was in no way getting on this man's back. But then, it was quite wet and…

Umph. The sky was suddenly upside down and rain pelted off my back instead of my head as my body bumped up and down. Freddie's hands were pressing firmly underneath my bottom, and when I finally came to the realization of what was happening, I was back on my own two feet outside the covered door of Lilian House B & B. I hadn't expelled an ounce of energy, but I was clear out of breath. Freddie, on the other hand, ran a block with me over his shoulders and looked as if he was out for a Sunday stroll. A wet Sunday stroll.

"I can't believe you just…"

"You're welcome," he replied stoically, running his hands through his wet hair.

I looked down at my shoes, which were still dry and void of any mud. He was right. I was quite thankful these beauties would live to see another club.

"Hmm… you know what? Thanks, actually. And, for the record, I *am* from Berkingsley. I just currently live in London."

"Well, Alice, from Berkingsley. Let's get you home, shall we?"

The day started pretty awful, but I couldn't help but look up into Freddie's somber eyes and feel a glimmer of hope. I didn't even roll my eyes when he teased, "Looks like I brought a pretty lady home with me after all."

CHAPTER 6

Hard Candy Christmas
(at the Local Food Market)

The music that played from the speakers in the ceiling of the M & S Food Hall must have been at least twenty years old, but it didn't stop me from joining in a duet with Santana as I strolled down the aisles. The rusty trolley wheels even seemed to grind to the beat as I pushed past the vast displays of produce decorating the store in tropical shades of orange, green, and yellow.

A little bit of this, a little bit of that... I sang as I added bag after bag of sugary treats, forming a stack that loomed over Pippy as she sat in the infant seat. Her curious little snout kept bobbing in the air, trying to sniff out the different scents we passed as we wandered through the candy aisle. Fizzy dummies, strawberry dewdrops, and lemon licorice torpedoes. *Can't forget the mint mentos, candy canes, or foam bananas. Mr. Fenk, the village dentist, is going to have my head after Santa brings all the children cavities for Christmas.*

Candy for the children, spirits for the grown-ups. A little something for everyone. A week had passed since we'd hashed out the details of our rescue plan over ale and nachos. We had quite the team assembled: a restaurant owner, a music teacher, a manager who supervised one of the biggest music halls in Europe, and an estate agent with lots of connections. It was the first time I truly gave thought to how driven and talented my friends were, and gosh, I was thankful for it.

This weekend was Berkingsley's annual Christmas market, an event that was nestled nostalgically in every resident's memory from childhood. It was a twist on the summer farmer's market, but instead of fruits and veggies, the multi-colored tents held tables of poinsettias and hot chocolate. Snow globes and wooden nutcrackers replaced wind chimes and kites. Colorful lights would be strung from tent to tent, and numerous umbrella heaters would be placed throughout the town center to keep both the vendors and the shoppers feeling cozy and warm. It was a magical experience for those few hours, and no one in town missed what we lovingly called the Berkingsley Christmas Festival.

Instead of enjoying the fun as spectators this year, we decided to contribute to it. Theo's father, a retired banker, often volunteered for the village council in his spare time and knew the chairman, Otto Gilman, quite well. Luckily, Theo's talkative personality came from his father, so we were hopeful his buoyant presentation would convince the council of our philanthropic intentions. We were a week past the deadline for vendor submissions, but Theo's dad had sold the committee with the promise of a Christmas market like no other. The committee also wanted to avoid the closure of a long-established business so beloved by the community. Our ideas were approved, with the stipulation that we submit a detailed write-up of our plan and also made the other businesses aware that the funds raised by our additions would be solely used to help the bookstore. No one could resist a charitable scheme, especially if it was laced with village gossip.

By the time the bags of sugar-crusted sweets filled the main basket of my grocery trolley, I was practically dancing down the aisles, riding the wave of enthusiasm prompted by the music and thoughts of saving the bookstore. I waltzed past buckets filled with flowers in various hues of pinks, reds, and whites and scooped up a petite bouquet of winter camellias sitting in a small mason jar, perfect for Mum. I raised it to my nose and inhaled the delicate fragrance, just a gentle hint of sweetness, barely there. I hoped it would work like a magic charm and spread my good mood onto her.

There she goes… there she goes again… I hummed along to the words sung by The La's coming from the ceiling and bent over to give Pippy a little nose-to-nose kiss. "It's a good day. Isn't it, Pips? It's a good day." The sign on the door had said in bold letters "Service Animals Only," but surely, no one could deny Pippy's entry when they saw what a sweet little girl she was.

The positive energy radiating off me suddenly turned to ash as a loud wail erupted from the floor in front of my trolley. "Blimey," I yelped as I attempted to slow the cho-reographed movement of the cart to a stop before colliding with whatever had thrown itself into a heap in front of me.

"EEEEEE!" a voice sobbed, and looking closer, I real-ized the full-on banshee call had come from the mouth of a small preschool-aged child.

"Dearie, what's wrong? Have you lost your mum?" I knelt next to the small boy, whose big green eyes were damp with tears.

He shook his head no and cried louder. "Oh dear," I said, shaking my head and beginning to panic sweat. I was not well-versed in these types of situations; the only maternal instinct I had at this point in my life came in the way of saving Pippy my pub leftovers.

"Should we go find someone who can help us?" I looked around the aisle, hoping to find someone more adult-ish than me, but the boy began crying louder, drawing my attention back. I guess this one was on me. I mustered up my confidence. I had worked as a receptionist at a five-star hotel for years and had advised a room full of businessmen just last month. I could handle a lost tot. "Oh, sweetie. It'll be alright. We'll find your mummy soon."

"She's not my mum. My mum's at work. I miss her." His sobs quieted as he wiped his snotty nose on the sleeve of his shirt.

"Oh, love. I understand. Here, let's get you a piece of candy, and then you can tell me who you came with." I turned to get a bag from my cart to share with the boy. Surely, a sweet treat would make him happy. But the boy, thinking I meant candy from the bulk containers beside him, pushed the spout holding hundreds of small fruit drops, and in an instant, a rush of hard candies poured down onto the floor. I threw myself toward the candy dispenser, trying to contain the chaos, but between the sound of my own voice yelling, the cries of surprise from the boy, and the hard echo of the candies hitting the linoleum floor, there was no way the commotion would go unnoticed. Pippy, alarmed by all the noise, high-jumped clear out of the cart and, in the process, knocked over my mother's flowers. The glass jar shattered into a thousand little pieces as it hit the floor.

I looked around at the mayhem, mouth gaping in stunned shock, and my body paralyzed momentarily. In the background of the mess, I could see Pippy trot away, but before I could do anything about it, a wiry voice called out.

"Oh, dear Lord, Charlie. I've been looking all over for you." A short elderly woman, holding a handbag on one arm and a basket on the other, tottered down the aisle, passing Pippy. She took in the scene before her and tsked. "What have you done, little boy? Nana is not happy."

The little guy, plopped on the floor in the middle of a maddening puddle of candies, was barely holding it together. His lower lip began to quiver, and the tears welled up again in his eyes. I could see the embarrassment and fear on his face, and even though I was no mother hen, I knew that shaming him would only make the situation worse.

"Oh, thank heavens, we found you, Mam'. Charlie, here, had stopped to say hello to my dog, and silly me, I let him down from the cart to pet. And next thing you know, we lost sight of you."

The old woman's eyes squinted with disbelief at my story, but before she could say anything, I continued. "And then, of course, my little pup decided to meddle with the candy dispensers, and oh goodness. What a mess!"

"Well, you should certainly take better care of your animal. Look at him wandering away." She gestured toward the end of the aisle, where Pippy turned back, stuck up her snout, and then continued trotting off. "Good heavens, why one would bring a dog into a market in the first place is beyond me. Charlie, come here this instant. Let's let this nice woman take care of her mess." The way she emphasized the word nice was anything but. She held her hand out and helped Charlie off the floor. As she pulled him toward the till, away from the candy and glass fragments, he looked back at me and gave a shy, apologetic smile. I winked and mouthed, "No worries, kiddo."

And then, there I was. Left with quite a mess. Biting my lip, I slowly nodded my head up and down, laughter bubbling out of me at the situation. A big, heartfelt chuckle of disbelief. What else was there to do?

"That's the spirit. Laughter is the best medicine, ain't it?"

I recognized that voice. It had been a week since I last saw him, but I knew that type of sarcasm could only belong to one man. I turned and saw Freddie, jeans hanging perfectly off his pelvis with a white sweater rolled up at his forearms, flaunting a tattoo of a lion holding a spear. In his arms was the little furry martyr herself, along with a package of beef jerky and a jar of peanut butter.

"Well, I'd say that I laugh in the face of danger, but that would be utterly untrue. I'm the first one to flee at the idea of anything remotely scary. But laughing at a floor covered in mint humbugs? That I can do with ease."

I tiptoed around the fragments of glass and took Pippy from his arms. I felt that zing of attraction that was becoming a common response to him as my hand brushed against the warmth of his skin. "Thank you for catching her before she wandered too far."

"So, this is the little champ that gets to eat like the Queen on your leftover takeaway," he said enthusiastically.

I stroked her fur over and over, probably a bit too aggressively than she was used to, but then again, she had never been used as a therapy dog before. And at that moment, my anxiety was flaring at a sky-high level. "Yes, this is the Queen herself. Freddie, meet Pippy. Pippy, Freddie." I lifted her little paw in salute. "What am I going to do? Will I forever be banned from the Food Hall? They have the best shrimp tempura in the village. This is a disaster."

"Nah, it's all taken care of. You'll be fine."

I laughed. "What do you mean, 'it's fine?' It looks like a robbery gone wrong. I'm so embarrassed."

"Come on, Alice. Grab your trolley, and let's go. I told you, it's all taken care of. I already informed the manager."

"Are you sure? My face won't appear on posters stapled to trees and bulletin boards around the neighborhood? This face is pretty recognizable, and I have quite a loud mouth, so people tend to know who I am around town. I don't want—

"Alice," he said abruptly. "Let's. Go." He took Pippy back from my arms, cradling her in his muscular arm and pushing the trolley with his other hand. I obligingly followed him, confused and slightly turned on by his ability to take command with two little words. I followed him innocently past the flower stand, where he stopped momentarily to pluck a ginormous floral bouquet from a bucket before continuing to the tills. My face grew hot in embarrassment as we approached the cashier. I tried thinking of the words to begin my apology. *Sir, I am utterly sorry…* No, not good enough. *Sir, you aren't going to believe what happened…* Hmm, sounds like I'm avoiding responsibility.

"Hello again, Angus." Freddie nodded at the middle-aged man at the register, whose name tag said *Manager*. "We'd like to ring up these packages of candy and this here bouquet, as well as my food. Again, my apologies for the mess back there."

"Ah, Freddie. Don't you worry 'bout a thing. I'll have my boys take care of it in no time. They've been a bit sluggish at their duties today, so this will help keep them on their toes." He was oddly happy for a man who'd just had his business ransacked. He grinned at Freddie so obnoxiously as he bagged the items that I was beginning to question his sanity.

"Thank you, Angus. See you around."

"Righto, Freddie." His eyes followed us as we walked past him and out the automatic doors.

When we reached the cobblestone sidewalk, Freddie squinted at me, the sun shining brightly today for a December afternoon.

"So, what's your plan with these?" He held up the bags filled to the top with candy. "Working Santa's wonderland again?"

I leaned down to clip Pippy's leash onto her collar. "Something like that." As I popped back up, I tilted my head at him inquisitively. "I don't know what kind of magic you made back there, but thank you."

"Ah, it was nothing compared to what you did for that little boy. Here." He removed the massive bouquet from the top of the bag, a mixture of roses, carnations, and others in gorgeous hues of purple, and held them out to me. "I couldn't help but notice your other ones just weren't up for the task."

"The task?" I asked.

"Yes. Of recognizing your kindness. Someone with a heart as good as yours deserves every damn single beautiful thing. Starting with this bouquet."

A shiver ran through my body, but it wasn't one of those discomforting ones caused by the chill in the air. It was a jolt of excitement, of warmth, and of anticipation for an unknown future.

I took the flowers from him, letting my fingers linger a second too long between his. "Well, thank you," I murmured. We stared at each other, both wondering what kind of thoughts were running through the other's head.

"Can I help you get all of this home?" he asked, ending the moment.

"Um, yes. Thank you. I'm just bringing them down to the bookstore, two blocks away. I had intended to take a few trips, but frankly, I don't want to show my face in that store for at least a week." I snorted. *Nice one, Alice.*

We began walking down the uneven sidewalk, side by side, with Pippy leading the way, her little legs working four times as hard to keep up the lead. Occasionally, our hands brushed each other's, and when they did, I couldn't keep my heart from fluttering in my chest.

"So, are you going to tell me what all of this candy is really for? Are you having some sort of party?"

"Well," I began, smiling. "Let me explain."

CHAPTER 7

Believe
(in New Love and the Fundraising Magic of Christmas Festivals)

The door of the eatery opened, pulling my attention away from the laptop on the table in front of me. Emilia glided in, wearing a thin peacoat over a day dress, earmuffs on her head. I was always after her for dressing inappropriately for the weather, but she claimed the winters here were nothing compared to Boston, where she grew up. I knew I'd be freezing my tits off if I dressed like her. At least she's wearing the wellies I bought her last year for her birthday.

"Hey, babe," I said in greeting as she sat down across from me at the rectangular table built for two. We were grabbing lunch at Mae's Eatery, Theo's restaurant. It was our favorite place to meet because of the fresh, modern farmhouse feel. Even in the dead of winter, light shone through the front panel of windows that spanned across the front of the building. Perfect for keeping that seasonal depression at bay. In the warmer months, the oversized windows propped open and a gorgeous flower display spanned across the short brown awnings outside. It was a favorite amongst locals and visitors alike.

"You're looking extra chipper today. I thought you said you were catching up on work before I got here," she said, nodding to the laptop that was now closed on the table.

"Oh, I was. I have some emails that still need attention and a client that is adamant about wearing a designer Rouje dress that I am having a hard time securing. But nothing I can't handle."

"How are you managing things from home? Is the agency getting by without you?"

"Well, you know, just barely. How does anyone get by without my talents?" I said, fluttering my eyelashes. I took a sip of my tea. "I'll be back at work by the end of next week. They'll survive without me. I'm also stopping in tomorrow to get caught up on some paperwork and deal with any minor fires that need extinguishing. Like, this Charlotte Diea woman. We are working to promote her company's new Italian perfume, and she's pushing back on the outfit that was chosen for the advertisement. Absolutely bonkers. But you know, my job is to keep the clients happy and all. Blah, blah, blah. I'll work my magic, though, and it will get sorted." I blew the bangs out of my eyes, releasing my frustration.

"It always does with you, my friend," Emilia said, placing her hand on top of mine and giving a quick squeeze.

"Ah, my girl finally arrived." Theo approached the table, giving Emilia a sweet kiss on the forehead, before dragging a seat over from a nearby table. He slung himself on the backward chair, resting his forearms on the top rail. He was dressed casually today in a long-sleeved green henley and jeans.

"Hi, baby. How's your day going?" Emilia asked, looking up at her guy with large doe eyes. Oh, these two. I couldn't even be jealous of their sappiness because they both meant so much to me. If anything, it encouraged my dreams about finding that kind of love. I thought I had it with Rian, but I obviously read that situation wrong.

"Not too bad. I've been cooped up in the office today, trying to assess our inventory and make sure the wine will be flowing freely on Saturday." Theo's role in the Christmas festival was an important one. The wine he served at his restaurant was from Chapel Farms, the local vineyard, and the same brand my parents sold in their shop. He would be keeping plenty of people warm and cheerful with wine tastings during the Christmas festival on Saturday. We also planned on having the bottles from Spines 'n' Wines on hand to sell. All of the money he raised from the wine tastings would be donated to the bookshop.

"Do you still need help selling the tickets for the tastings? Julia offered to help if needed," Emilia asked. Julia was the receptionist at Blackley Manor who took over for me when I finished my fashion degree and dived headfirst into the marketing world.

"Nah, Stewart is helping me serve, and Scarlett is going to sell the tickets. We should be all set. Thanks, love." He drummed the table before standing.

"I'm so glad big sis is coming back into town to help with the event. We need a little bit of her contemptuous authority to ensure this all works out," I said.

"Yes, I agree 100 percent with that. Scarlett will be a huge help all weekend," Theo replied before changing subjects. "Are you ladies feeling like your usual for lunch? Or shall I surprise you with my own personal creation?"

"Oh, nope," I groaned. "I'm not falling for that again. That leek salad tasted like shite last time. Shite, tossed in lemon vinaigrette and topped with cheese. I like cheese as much as the next girl, but all the cheese in the world couldn't fix that dish," I jabbered.

"Hey, that was a Theo Original. I had to use up some of my veggies before they went bad." He flashed a wink at Emilia.

"Oh, I doubt that, sir. You just like torturing me. I do know how to give a review on Yelp, so you'd better watch yourself."

"Ouch, Alice. Alright, I'll have Stewart make you the usual chicken salad sandwich. No tricks this time. But probably shouldn't leave a Yelp review anyway. Seems a bit unethical, family and all."

"You might like playing the role of big brother Theo, but last time I checked, we had different parents. Better make that sandwich extra tasty. With a big pickle on the side. And some crisps."

His eyebrows raised as he smirked back at me. "One tasty sandwich with a big pickle coming up. And, for you, my love?" He looked over at Emilia. "Theo's special?"

Emilia shook her head. "I'm with Alice on this one. I'll just have the garden salad with some bread.

With a shrug of his shoulders, he began his walk back to the kitchen. "Your loss, ladies. You're missing something good."

"Oh, and honey?" Emilia called out, stopping Theo in his tracks. "I'd also love a caramel latte, with a special surprise foam design." She giggled.

He smiled at that, before responding, "Anything for you, love."

"I sure hope you don't let that man cook for you at home," I jested once Theo returned to the kitchen.

"Surprisingly, he can make some delicious meals. I think you're right. He just likes pulling your leg." She readjusted her long, blonde hair into a high ponytail, a small smirk on her face.

"Always has. I thought maybe he'd cut me some slack when he became engaged to my best friend, but I guess that's just a pipe dream. I'm so glad you could meet for lunch, anyhow. I have so much to tell you." I leaned across the table, my hands under my chin, bubbling with excitement. "Remember Freddie, the guy I had a drink with at the pub last week?" My eyes lit up so big that Emilia probably thought I was on something. "I bumped into him at the grocery store yesterday, and well, I might not be going back there after the absolute shite storm Pippy and I created. But anyway, he found me there, sitting with a million pieces of hard candy and glass everywhere, yet he didn't hide, and he somehow fixed the whole situation.

The manager didn't even bat an eye. He was so transfixed on Freddie that he didn't even make me pay for the mess." My eyebrows scrunched in puzzlement. "Which, come to think of it, is quite odd. I mean, Freddie *is* pretty hot, but to be that mesmerized by him just seems a bit overkill…"

Emilia made a stop sign with her hand, interrupting my soliloquy. "Hold up, Alice." Her cheeks bubbled up in an attempt to hold back a grin. "I have no idea what you are going on about, but I heard the name Freddie multiple times, and I haven't seen you this excited about a man since your plan to find me a hookup last year."

"Totally Em, and rightly so. He is freaking hot. Capital H hot. Like, melt an ice cube down those abs, hot."

Emilia coughed up the water that she had just swallowed. "Um, what? You've seen him naked? You forgot to tell me that small detail."

"Sadly, no," I pouted. "Not yet, at least. But I can just imagine what he has hidden under his shirt if those forearms and jawline indicate anything." My lower lip puckered at Emilia's response. "I'll take that laughter as agreement, missy."

"Oh, sure. There is definitely a direct correlation between a six-pack and a defined jawline. Do tell me more about this absolute stud of a man."

I ignored her sarcasm and eagerly continued. "He's quiet and reserved, but he asks me questions about myself like he wants to know more. And not just your typical small-talk questions."

"Alice, honey, that's what a guy is supposed to do when he's interested in you."

"Yeah, well, it just seems like it's been a while since someone took an interest in who I am beyond my looks."

"As they should. You have so much to offer, and truthfully, you don't need a man to tell you that you are amazing. You just need to see it yourself. Miss Gorgeous Fashion Consultant with a head of brains and a heart as big as your closet. Rian stole your confidence when he left, and that zealous, larger-than-life girl that we all love has gotten a bit weathered."

I nodded, feeling the tears build in my eyes. I hadn't felt like myself these last few months, and Emilia was pinpointing exactly what I had been feeling but hadn't been able to put into words. I swiped my finger under my eye. No need to ruin a good makeup day. "Relationships bloody suck."

Emilia laughed. "Yes, they do. And they are freaking complicated. Remember, you were the one who encouraged me to step outside my comfort zone and start a relationship with Theo, even when I was terrified to commit to something outside my music. And now I'm telling you, you don't need a man. You are one hell of a woman on your own. But if you want one, well, find one that treats you right. Sounds like this Freddie guy might be one of those. But you do need to tell me more first, beyond the very obvious fact that he looks like a sex God."

I eagerly spilled the details of yesterday afternoon, starting with the candy incident and the hour that followed. Freddie had helped me bring all the candy back to the bookstore and then we went for a walk around the village. Turns out Pippy had snuck a few pieces of candy and had some energy to burn off, and we didn't want to say goodbye so soon. Freddie asked me all about my parents' store and what my plans were to help get them back on their feet. We talked about our favorite Christmas traditions (mine was drinking non-alcoholic wassail with Scarlett as a kid while Dad and Mom put on a spectacular retelling of The Night Before Christmas, and his involved hour-long snowball fights with his sisters), which breakfast food we couldn't live without (poached eggs on toast for him—blech—and banana french toast for me), and how we would survive if the internet suddenly broke (short answer—I'd be lost somewhere down an alley in London). He loved to ask me these random questions, scrunching his eyebrows at my response before nodding his head in acknowledgment. His answers were short, but he'd look at me after I'd share mine, like he was pondering every point I made, really giving it thought like I was some eighteenth-century philosopher. And, if you knew me, you knew I loved the attention.

Once we realized we would both be in London at the same time on Thursday, we agreed to meet up in the early evening to do some last-minute Christmas shopping and grab dinner. I had to admit, I was really looking forward to seeing him.

After Em and I finished our lunch, which Theo thankfully kept his paws away from, we said our goodbyes. I had one more stop before heading back to the hotel. I had promised I would help Dad with something at the shop, and I also needed to pick Pippy up. Mum was out on her weekly lunch date with her lady friends, so I knew Pippy would be safe from being dropped at the local pound. As the bookshop door slammed shut behind me, I called out, "Dad, I'm here."

"By the fire, Alice," his gentle voice said from the corner. I walked down the row of thrillers and sci-fi novels and found him sitting in the brown armchair by the fire, my sleeping fluff ball on his lap. One hand stroked Pippy's back methodically, over and over, while the other extended over the armrest, a pipe securely resting in its palm.

"Dad, ew. You really shouldn't be smoking that. Mum will kill ya if it doesn't end you first. Plus, it's stinking up the place." I sat down next to him in the adjacent chair, waving my hand dramatically in the air.

He put the pipe between his lips and sucked in, holding the smoke inside for a few seconds before exhaling. Clearly not getting the message. "Some people find the smell comforting. It brings back fond memories of my pa smoking every night. You know, we only have about two more months left here, Alice. I'm sure you've heard that the damage and cleanup were more than we can manage. We didn't want to tell you until after Christmas, but you know your mum's friends. It's hard to believe that they once were the biggest secret keepers in the village."

His voice delivered the devastating news with the evenness of a rolling pin. But my hopeful heart only beat faster with excitement. "About that, Dad. I have this plan to—"

His voice changed tone, and the smoothness that usually defined it turned coarse. "Alice, stop. I know about your plans. That can't be a surprise. And it's a noble gesture. I know your giving heart always wants to help others with their troubles, but this is one thing that you can't fix. Your ma and I have discussed it, and we won't be taking any handouts."

"But, Dad—"

He raised his hand to stop any more words from leaving my mouth. I sank into the seat, retreating back to the role of indignant child. It's funny that no matter how many digits get added on to your age or how many corporations trust your opinion on how best to market their products, when you are back in your childhood home, facing a lecture from one of your parents, you suddenly transform into that sullen eight-year-old kid.

"You know, my pa died from black lung disease, but it wasn't from the pipes he smoked. He worked in the coal mines of Bristol from a young age until the year that he died. It was grueling work. When he turned the pages of the books he read to us late at night, I would notice his stained fingertips and worry that he would soil my favorite stories."

The flames from the fireplace reflected off his eyes as he stared solemnly into the light, rubbing the gray stubble on his face. "No matter how hard he scrubbed, the dust remained. I hadn't given any thought to what it did to his lungs, even when he'd keel over in coughing fits." He turned toward me. "And then one day, he died. And I grew up. I met your mum and found myself on the very same path as my pa, with a wife to support and dreams of raising a family. I worked long hours and saved every penny, and your mum took in people's laundry and also worked harder than she should've. But we only had to do this for a few years. We found this building for pennies by total luck and God's blessing, and we knew it would be perfect for a bookstore. A place where we could remember the sacrifices my pa made for me, my mum, and your aunt.

"I'm sorry, Dad. I never knew. You've never told me these stories. And Aunt Lily, well, she seemed so well-off when she came to visit. I had no idea of the struggles your family endured."

"We all do what we need to survive. Your aunt married a fella who happened to have a lot of wealth but later learned that he gained it outside the perimeters of the legal system. Your mum and I chose a different path. We were resilient. We made sacrifices. We built this shop from our hard work and choices. And then we had your sister and you, and it all suddenly made good sense."

He stopped stroking Pippy's fur and held his hand out to me. I took the rough yet fatty palm in mine and gave it a squeeze. "So, you see. We don't want charity. We began this on our own terms, and we'll see it to the end our own way."

I nodded my head as my dad's words came to an end.

"I understand, Dad. I really do. I know you still see me as your little girl, and I always will be, but I'm a grown woman now. You don't need to worry about Scarlett or me anymore. You've done it for so long. It's time for you and Ma to let others take care of you."

I swallowed the lump in my throat. I hadn't meant to share this on this visit home when the wound was still fresh. But here it goes. "You know, Rian and I broke up. A few months ago, actually." I stared at him, waiting for a reaction, but he merely nodded his head.

Finally, he broke the silence. "Your mother would want to know."

I looked down sheepishly, suddenly ashamed of my omission. "I know."

He took another long puff on his pipe. Even though he had just opened up to me, he wasn't one to discuss emotions, especially ones that involved the men I was seeing. "Are you okay?" he asked.

"Yeah, I'm okay. At first, I didn't tell you because it hurt too much to discuss it, but then I didn't want to disappoint you and Mum. I know how much you loved Rian."

He sighed. "Alice, it wasn't Rian that we loved so much as it was seeing you so happy."

Nodding my head, I replied, "And a part of me knows that. The point I'm trying to make is that we all try to hide our feelings from each other, not wanting to upset or disappoint the ones we love. But we are family, Dad. If we can't trust each other with all of our messes, then who can we turn to?"

"You and Mum are lucky." I continued. "Your family extends far beyond Scarlett and me. Your neighbors, the friends you've grown up with, the customers who visit every week looking for recommendations on what to read next—they love you. You've helped so many through tough times with a mere suggestion of a book title. And hell, if that didn't work, you paired it with a bottle of wine. Now's the time to let them—let *us*— help you."

He stroked the whiskers on his chin, seemingly contemplating the words of wisdom his youngest daughter surprisingly dealt. "I'll talk it over with your mum. But only if you talk to her about Rian."

Unbelievable. Did I just get my stubborn father to consider changing his mind on something? I felt like I needed to do something physical to seal the deal, like a handshake or a hug. Maybe a signed document? Something to ensure he upheld his end of the deal. But before I could figure out what would work best, the bookstore door opened.

I gave Dad a quick kiss on the cheek, followed by a thank you whispered into his ear. "I'll handle the customer if you handle the little one." I gave a slight nod at Pippy as he tamped the end of the pipe and tried to dissipate the smell with a frantic wave of his hand, probably fearing his life in case it was Mum who entered the door. He quickly got up from his chair and scurried upstairs.

CHAPTER 8

My Favorite Things
(and Nana's too)

Lucky for him, it wasn't Mum. "Why, hello." I greeted the family at the door with a big, genuine smile. I felt a bit lighter now that I had finally disclosed my relationship status and the secrecy that accompanied it. A beautiful black woman in her early thirties with short, curly hair stood at the front of the store, holding a wiggly toddler in her arms. "Here, Mummy," the young girl standing beside her said as she slipped off her jacket and held it out for her mother to add to her already overfilled arms.

The girl bounced over to me, her pigtails bobbing up and down with each movement. She looked to be about six or seven. She reached into the unicorn rucksack she held in her hands and removed a purple pencil and a pad of paper. "Hi, I'm looking for…" Her eyebrows scrunched in deep concentration as she flipped through the pages of her notebook for her answer. "A Miss Alice. Would that be you?" She looked up at me like she was about to give an interrogation about a neighborhood crime.

I replied with all the seriousness I could muster. Clearly, this girl was on a mission. "That would be me. How may I be of help?"

She tapped the pencil on her chin. "Yes, I was told that you would be able to find a suitable present for my nana. Here are her interests: bird watching, baking pies, knitting—quite terribly, but don't tell her I said that—and vacuuming. Do you have anything that fits these descriptions?"

I pretended to give it some thought, then finally answered, "Why, yes. I believe I do. Why don't you follow me?"

I met her mum's gaze and smiled as she mouthed back, "Thank you."

"So, is this a gift for your nana? Is it for Christmas or a birthday, perhaps?"

"Christmas," she responded. "I have only two people left on my list." She looked back to make sure her mother wasn't too close and then whispered, "I already got my mum an assortment of tea. She loves to drink a cuppa each morning while making me breakfast. It has so many flavors: peach, mint, mango, green…"

"Sounds like it has all the flavors of the rainbow. I think your mum will be so surprised." The precocious girl marched behind me like a proud soldier as I led her back to the bookshelf filled with an assortment of non-fiction titles. Her mum followed a bit behind, letting her little boy toddle around the rows of shelves. "Here are a few books about bird watching, and over here is a wonderful cookbook filled with dessert recipes for every day of the year."

The girl's eyes lit up. "Oh, wow. I think she'd love that. I'm her taste tester, you know. I have a notebook where I rate everything she bakes from one to ten. Most everything is a ten, except for when she puts raisins in the mix. Then it's an immediate two."

I knelt and pulled the cookbook off the shelf. "Yes, I 100 percent understand how that would make any dessert a two. I don't think there are too many recipes in here that involve raisins, but I do know there are a lot that have chocolate, others that have raspberries, and some that have both!" It seemed that this little girl and I shared a sweet tooth.

She pondered my words for a second before nodding her head and putting a big checkmark in her notebook. "This will be perfect. Thank you. I have one more gift I need to get. This one is for my Uncle Freddie. He's the one who told me that if I came here, you'd be able to help me. But since you know him, you must promise not to tell what I pick for him."

My cheeks puffed up in a smile. This cheeky little girl was Freddie's niece. What an adorable little muffin. "Your uncle is my friend, huh?"

Her mum's voice responded behind me. "Freddie told us all about you, which is no small feat for my brother. He's a man of few words, which I'm sure you know."

I stood up from my place on the floor and stuck my hand out like an animal sticking its head between the fence at a petting zoo. "I met Freddie a couple of weeks ago. I'm so glad he told you to stop in. I'm sorry I didn't introduce myself sooner. I'm Alice."

"I'm Sophie, and that there is Andrew." She nodded at her son who was now playing with the train set circling the Christmas tree.

"And I'm Elizabeth, but you can call me Liddy." The little girl stuck her hand out, making sure she was still a part of the conversation.

"Funny that you just met Freddie. He spoke like he knew you quite well. He seemed pretty confident that you could help this one here." She nodded at her daughter.

"That I absolutely can do. Now, tell me, Liddy, what sorts of things does your Uncle Freddie like?"

She wrinkled her nose. "Well, he likes football and ale…"

"Just like every other man in England, I suppose," Sophie jokingly said to me. "I promise there is more to my brother than sports and beer. Dearie, what else does Uncle Freddie like to do?"

"He likes to toss Andrew in the air over and over. Oh, and he likes to draw with me!"

"Ah, well, that's it, then. I have just the thing for him," I reply. "Follow me." We walked over to the children's section. "Let's see," I said as I ran my finger across the books on the shelf. "Here it is. *Our Doodling Journal*. This is a special notebook that you can share with your Uncle Freddie. You can draw and write back and forth. It's kind of like a gift for you and him!"

She eagerly pulled the book from my hands and brought it to her chest in a hug. Her excitement couldn't be any bigger if I had promised her a puppy. "Mum, Uncle Freddie was right. Alice is really smart and good at her job, and she's just as pretty as he said."

"Oh, well, thank you." I laughed. *So, Freddie thinks I'm smart and pretty? Well, how about that?* My feelings were quite reciprocal, although pretty might not be the first word that comes to my mind when I thought about him. I tried to change the direction that my thoughts were heading before the heat on my cheeks gave me away.

"Here, Mum." She handed both books over. "My shopping is done. I'm going over to play with Andrew and the train. Thank you, Miss Alice."

"Not a problem, darling. Happy Christmas." I watched her skip away.

"Freddie tells me this is your parents' bookstore?" Sophie asked, the two of us suddenly free from children. "What a clever concept to include wine and spirits alongside books. Usually, you see books and tea paired together, not alcohol."

"Yes, well, I always thought it was a shame that it wasn't a bookstore with an actual working bar. That would make for a relaxing experience, and I'm sure it would help us sell a few more books."

She laughed. "It's quite surprising that it isn't a thing. I know my sister, Nella, attends a monthly wine social disguised as a book club. She swears they have lengthy discussions about the books, but I know my sister, and I'm pretty sure that she hasn't picked up anything remotely resembling a book in years."

"Well, bring her in here. I'll get her hooked on the newest Abby Jimenez release. Her romcoms have never failed to woo a customer."

"I will! And if I can't convince her, I'm sure Liddy will create a list of reasons why she should stop in."

Her smile was so easygoing that I felt like we were already fast friends. She was pretty much a picture of sophisticated zen. Even bungled down with a diaper bag, children's jackets, and the two books Liddy picked out, her hair was perfectly set, and she showed no signs of frenzy that usually accompanied the parents that wandered into the store. I hadn't even noticed that her eyes were rotating surveillance cameras. She gave the illusion that her full attention was on me until she abruptly backtracked toward the tree and stopped her son from derailing the entire train set. "Andrew, dear, please leave the train on the tracks."

"Choo-Choo, go," he responded, trying to lift the caboose off the tracks, knocking the rest of the train on its side.

"Andrew, Mummy said no. Come on, dear. Let's put this right and go say goodbye to our new friend, Alice." She began to set the train upright, and Liddy joined in.

"Don't worry about the train," I said to Sophie. "I can fix it later." I scrunched down to the floor and said to the kids, "Why don't you both come to the till with me? I have a little surprise for you."

"I love surprises. Come on, Andrew." She reached her hand out to her brother, and he placed his little one in hers, letting her slowly lead the way to the front of the shop. What darling children.

I reached down into the drawer behind the counter. "Let's see. I have bookmarks and stickers. Which would you prefer?" I asked them, holding up a bookmark with safari animals hiding in a jungle with a caption that said,

"Reading opens the door to adventures" and a sticker with a pile of smiling rocks that stated, "Reading Rocks."

"I'll have the bookmark. Thank you." She turned to her little brother, and he pointed eagerly to the sticker. "And he'll take the sticker."

"And I'll take these two books and this bottle of red," Sophie chimed in, setting a bottle of cabernet on the counter. "This is a wonderfully inviting space. I hope your parents manage to keep it open. Freddie told me all about the plumbing issues and your efforts to raise money to cover the costs. I'll be sure to tell my friends to stop in. We live just outside the village, in the town of Reading. But we grew up in the margins of Berkingsley. My brother and I are probably a tad older than you, but you might know my youngest sister, Lulu Carter, from secondary school."

"Hmm, her name sounds familiar, but I can't quite place her face. I hadn't realized that you all attended the same school as me! Freddie and I never discussed it. It's nice to have that shared feeling of home, though, isn't it? I currently live in the city, but there's nothing like being back home in the village."

"Agreed. We come out here often since it's so close. I love that the kids are getting familiar with the village I grew up in." She scooped up the paper bag I slid across the counter in her arms, lifting Andrew a second later. I walked around the counter and handed Liddy her books.

"I thought you'd want to put these in your school bag. Help your mummy out." I put my hand up to my mouth as if to tell her a secret, just between her and me, although

I kept my voice audible for her mum to hear. "You don't want anyone to see them before you can wrap them up."

Her eyes widened in agreement as she shoved them into her bag, gaily bobbing her head up and down. "It was a pleasure to meet you, Miss Alice." She took her mother's hand and tugged her toward the door. I had no idea how Sophie could juggle so many things in her arms at once. I pulled the door open for the sprightly little group and said my goodbyes.

"Thanks again, Alice. I hope to see you soon," Sophie said. "I'll tell Freddie to bring you by the house," she added so nonchalantly that it took me a moment to comprehend what she had said. Before I could protest and remind her that Freddie and I were just newly acquainted, she was out the door into the brisk afternoon air.

Well, that was a pleasant little surprise. I grabbed my mobile and found the contact for Freddie that he gave me the other day when we exchanged numbers.

> **ME:** So, rumor has it that I'm really smart and the best bookseller around, huh?

>> **FREDDIE (BOOKSTORE DUKE):** ...?

>> **FREDDIE (BOOKSTORE DUKE):** I mean, yes, you most definitely are. But also ...?

> **ME:** I just had the most adorable little girl in pigtails as a customer tell me so.

FREDDIE (BOOKSTORE DUKE): Aww, did Sophie bring the kids by?

ME: Yes, and I have never been so nervous to recommend the wrong book to a seven-year-old.

FREDDIE (BOOKSTORE DUKE): She's six.

ME: Ha. Of course. What a smart little thing.

FREDDIE (BOOKSTORE DUKE): She takes after her uncle.

ME: I'm sure…

Do I send a winky face? Is that too presumptuous? Oh, what the hell.

ME: 😉

FREDDIE (BOOKSTORE DUKE): What secrets did they disclose about me?

ME: Oh, lots. But I pinky promised that I wouldn't say.

FREDDIE (BOOKSTORE DUKE): Are we still on for tomorrow evening?

ME: Most definitely.

FREDDIE (BOOKSTORE DUKE): I wasn't sure after they told you all my secrets.

The dotted typing lines scrolled across the screen, followed by a pause. And then more dots.

FREDDIE (BOOKSTORE DUKE): I'm looking forward to it.

ME: ~~You are?~~

Delete… delete… delete…

ME: Me too. ☺

CHAPTER 9

Happy Xmas – War is Over
(with Work Clients and my Sister)

I sat at my desk early the next afternoon, feeling cautiously optimistic. The view had nothing to do with it. The office of a new(ish) fashion marketer was about the size of a closet and not the fancy walk-in type. If that wasn't cringe-worthy enough, I also shared the room with my super-talented partner, Evelyn, who was currently on a late lunch break. Her degree was also in fashion and marketing, so we did our best to make the room as chic as possible, adding a few framed paintings and fake plants since we had no windows for living ones. My desk supplies, from the stapler to the file holder, all matched in a beautiful teal hue, and the yellow sunshine rug I put at my feet helped remind me of the presumably bright skies outside, although I knew that was an unlikely truth on a winter day in London.

After a lengthy video call, I had finally convinced

Charlotte Diea that her model would look just as stunning in a flowing skirt as she would in the pantsuit she had originally set her mind on. I reminded her that someone standing on a boat, staring into a sunset, probably would not be dressed like she was going to the office, and the imagery I described seemed to satisfy her.

A solid three-knuckled-knock vibrated on my office door before Sheila poked her head in. Sheila was the head of our creative department and had an exceptionally kind and understanding personality for such a high-pressure position. She also had the work speed of a baby cheetah, darting here and there, gone in a flash before you had an opportunity to ask her questions. But she made sure shite got done and had been patient with me as I learned all the new ins and outs of my position in the last year.

"Hello, Alice. Thanks for stopping in today to clear up some issues. Did the Diea problem get solved?"

"Yes, we are full speed ahead with that campaign. Everything should be ready for next week. I've also drawn up social media plans for next month's Stella McCartney's ad campaign."

"That's my girl. Working magic, I see. Before you leave today, please check in with Evelyn to ensure all is set for tomorrow's photo shoot for the new Firsch Co. line."

"Will do. And Sheila?" I said, stopping her before she continued on her frenzied way. She turned back, "Yes?"

"Thank you for making me take these last couple of weeks off. You were right. I needed them, and when I return next week, I know my focus will be 100 percent on the job."

She pinched her lips together, pausing to think before replying. "I'm glad, Alice. It may have been many years ago, but I was your age once. I remember how earth-shattering your first real heartbreak feels. But this was a one-and-done exception. Don't presume I will be as patient next time. And, of course, you'll be giving up next year's holiday hours until you accumulate the time back."

"Of course, Sheila. I understand. That's only fair."

The crinkle in her eyebrows dissolved into a quick, warm smile. "I'm happy to see you today, and the work you've done from home has been impressive. Keep it up."

I nodded my head. "Thank you, Sheila."

She was gone in an instant, and I was left to fret over whether that was a positive interaction or if I'd soon be tasked with brewing the office coffee. *Positive.* I told myself. *Definitely positive.* I was a hard worker, and I knew I could earn back all of Sheila's trust and respect from the effort I put forth. I pushed any lingering negative thoughts to the back of my mind. I quickly glanced at my mobile to see if my parents had gotten back to me about the fundraising plan. Even though Dad said he'd talk it over with Ma, I hadn't received a reply yet from either of them. The Christmas Festival was in two days, and it was pretty much full speed ahead from here. I was really hoping they were hopping on board the train so we could avoid a train wreck. But there were no messages or voicemails from them. I gathered up my files and laptop and secured them in my work bag. Evelyn should be back any minute, and then I planned on heading to my London flat to check on things.

As I sorted through the mail from the last week on my little dining table, all that greeted me were mostly bills and a few fashion magazines. I audibly cheered at the sight of a Christmas card and eagerly tore it open when my mobile buzzed. I swiped right.

"Hi, big sis! What's been going on this week?"

Silence the likes of a church sanctuary greeted me back.

"Um, hellooooo? Did you butt-dial me?"

I heard the click of her nails rolling across a table in the background. I knew what that meant. I walked over to the sink in my kitchen and filled a glass with water.

"Are you giving me the silent treatment? *You* are the one who called me, you know." I poured the water into the house plants on my windowsill, trying to maintain my good mood by breathing in the fresh oxygen the little guys emitted.

Still, silence.

"Oh, crikey. If you aren't going to tell me what's been going on, then I'm hanging up now. I don't have the energy for this."

Her voice blasted from my mobile speaker, spitting with anger. "What's been going on *this week*? How about, what's been going *on the last few months*? You tell me, *little sis*. Because you obviously have forgotten to do so."

I groaned into the phone. She knew. "You found out. Ma told you?"

"Told me that you and Rian broke up months ago? That you've been moping around and even were forced on a leave of absence at work because of it? That you haven't shared the news with anyone and have been dealing with all the post-break-up shite by yourself? Yes, she told me. And yeah, I'm infuriated you didn't tell me."

"It wasn't a leave of absence, and Emilia knew, and… wait… *you're* mad?" I wasn't planning on dragging this up, but my emotions bubbled up like a volcano on the verge of erupting. "Okay, Miss Hotshot. Why did *you* keep the news about the bookstore a secret? I had a right to know it was closing soon. That's our home. It might've hurt a little less if I had heard it from you instead of the gossip from ladies in the village."

Scarlett sighed on the other end of the call. Both our emotions were running at a sprint, and even though we were miles away, the tension in the room could cut like a knife. Scarlett and I had a complicated relationship. I loved her and have always looked up to her. But she went through some hard times and closed herself off from me for a few years. We had lived and worked together at Blackley Manor for years, but our relationship wasn't as close as it had been when we were younger. We shared things, but sometimes it was just too damn hard, and we often took the easier route and avoided the emotional conversations until they boiled over…like today.

"Alice, I'm so deeply sorry for that. I'm ashamed, actually. But Ma and Dad made me promise. They didn't want you to know before the holidays. They requested one last Christmas where we could pretend things were normal. I knew it was the wrong choice, but they wouldn't listen to me. I swear."

I half laughed, half huffed. "Yeah, that sounds a lot like Dad's stubbornness and Ma's sentimentality at play."

"Yup, he's like me, and there is so much in you from Ma. I'm sorry. I really am. That's why I agreed last week to come home and help with the Christmas market. I'm proud of you, sis. Here I thought I was the event-planning hospitality gal in the family, but it looks like I have an equal partner now."

My voice grew vulnerable. "I'm glad you're coming home, Scarlett. I need you here. I'm scared it won't work out and that it won't be enough. Dad and Ma haven't even agreed to let us help yet."

"I just spoke with them, and it sounds like they finally gave us their blessing."

My hand flew to my mouth, and I grew giddy with relief. "That makes me so happy. I've put so much work into making this event a success. I was afraid they were going to put a stop to it before we even had a chance to try."

"We'll make it work. We'll do our damn best, at least. And that's all we can do at this point."

"You're right. We'll give it the ole' Evans Girl attempt, and hopefully, that will be enough," I said.

"Now, tell me all about the breakup. I'm here to listen and help in any way I can."

I plopped myself down on my sofa, surrounding myself with my emotional-support pillows. I hadn't spoken in detail to anyone besides Emilia, and that was weeks ago. But it felt therapeutic to talk it over with Scarlett. I noticed that when I described the moment Rian dropped the breakup bomb on me, it didn't hurt as much anymore. It was after we had watched our favorite reality show together, snuggled on the couch, eating our usual Tuesday night Thai takeaway. *He knew how to ruin some of my favorite things, that shitehead.* But I couldn't hate him any longer. Even though he broke my heart, it belonged to him for a long time. He didn't do it in the best way, but he was always awkward when it came to hard things, and honestly, when you've been in a relationship for that long, there was never going to be an easy way to break up.

"Alice, it sounds like maybe you're starting to be okay. If there's one thing I've learned from the heartbreaking pieces of my past, it's that even if things aren't meant to be forever, it doesn't mean that they weren't supposed to happen at all. Your relationship with Rian will forever be a part of who you are, and it was what you needed at the time. But now you're in a new chapter of your life, and you'll find your way. I know you will. You always have."

"Thanks, sis. I'm glad you called. I'm sorry for not telling you."

"It's okay. I'm sorry, too. In the future, let's both try to let each other in sooner."

"Well, I do have some news to share. I might have somewhat of a date tonight…"

ME: So, surprise! I finished work early and decided to grab the best hot ham and cheese sandwich to share with you. Also picked up an order of cheese fries, but I might have already devoured them before the taxi showed up. #Sorrynotsorry.

ME: What's your address? Are you done with work yet?

FREDDIE (BOOKSTORE DUKE): Great! Yes, I'm just about finished. It's Fulham Road, Fulham, SW6 1HS. Ring when you get here so I can come get you.

ME: On my way. I'll see you soon.

CHAPTER 10

All I Want for Christmas is You
(and a Couple Thousand Dollars)

A s the black taxi pulled up to the address, I hopped out of the vehicle and looked up at the buildings towering over me. Was this the right place? I guess in all of our chats, we never talked specifics about what we did for work in London. But surely, this wasn't the correct address. *Oh, bonkers. Just my luck.* I sent a message to Freddie asking him to resend the address.

> **ME:** You'll never believe where the taxi left me off. It's nuts.

I put my mobile back in my purse and turned back to get into the taxi, but the driver had already pulled away.

A smooth voice ahead called, "Nuts, really?" I looked up and there was Freddie, standing in athletic pants, a zipped-up sports jacket, and a black beanie. I did a dou-ble-take. He looked smoking hot in his athleisure gear.

"So, I guess we forgot to share what we do during our 9-5 grind. What *do* you do here? I mean, Stamford Bridge? Isn't this where they hold football games or something?"

"Yeah. It's the stadium for Chelsea F.C." He motioned for me to walk ahead with him.

"Oh, well, that's pretty neat. What do you do here?" Poor guy. I knew it was hard getting a job with a background in history, but selling concessions seemed like a tough break.

He chuckled to himself. "Come on, Alice. I'm going to show you." As we walked up the sidewalk, the images of football players lined the painted wall of the entrance. It was pretty void of crowds at the moment, but a few secu-rity guards were patrolling around. As we passed one, he nodded his head at Freddie. I gave him a warm smile and looked up ahead at the images.

"Holy shite, Freddie." I stopped in my tracks. My mouth flew open, and my eyes expanded like flying saucers. I pointed at him. Then, at the wall. Then back at him. "Is that YOU? Are you a football player? What the–"

He reached over with his hand and lifted my chin back up to my mouth. His eyebrows joined his mouth in a play-ful smirk before shrugging his shoulders in slow motion.

"Yeah, I guess I am. Is that okay?"

"Well, yeah. I guess. I mean, of course. I mean… wow." I took a deep breath. I had zero interest in sports. I didn't even know the rules of football, except you couldn't use your hands. I mean, duh. It's in the name. So, I can't say that I was starstruck. Mostly, just surprised. And a little turned on. I don't know how it was possible, but he even looked hotter, blown up four times his size. His thick thighs sat snug in his uniform and every strand of muscle was visible in the photo. His eyes darkened in intense concentration as he flew through the air, kicking the ball high in the air.

My body froze as it tried to catch up with my rambling brain, but with a point of his finger, Freddie bypassed the awkward moment. "Are you going to share that sandwich with me? I'm pretty famished after practice."

"Um, yeah." I handed over the paper bag that held our meals. "They're most likely cold but I promise, still worth every bite."

He pulled out a sandwich, handed me one, and unwrapped the end of the other, taking a huge bite as we walked toward the stadium. Enormous blue banners cascaded down the sides of the building, and there, front and center stood a statue of a man holding a football in his hand. I followed Freddie around the side of the building to a black door, where he swiped a keycard and let us in.

"Thanks for bringing food. This hit the spot." He tossed the wrapper into a nearby trash bin. "How was your day at the office?"

So, that's how it was going to be. We weren't going to discuss this huge boulder that sat between us. And it was pretty massive. Freddie was a football player for Chelsea? I couldn't wrap my head around it. But it was obvious he didn't want it to be a big deal. So, I pretended it wasn't. While he gave me a tour of the stadium where he played his games, I smiled and nodded my head. He told me it was rare that he practiced here, but they had an open practice special for the holiday season this morning. The field looked infinite, and it was hard to imagine him down there, playing before crowds of screaming fans. A chill ran down my spine just looking down from the seats at the turf that produced a magnificent hue of green under the flares of the lights. With the clouds holding an effervescent shimmer as dusk fell, it was an eerie sort of beautiful, being the only two people in this palace built for thousands.

"I never thought I would say a football field was breathtaking, but here I am. It's beautiful, Freddie."

The left side of his mouth lifted in a half-smile as his eyes left the field and caught mine. "It's a different beast down there on the pitch. So, I appreciate it when someone can remind me just how magical the scene can be from the stands. Come on, let me show you more." He reached for my hand as we climbed down the stands, both leading the way and making sure I didn't stumble in my heels.

We walked through a tunnel and passed an area with cushioned tables and plastic tubs where the players received physical therapy and ice baths, and finally, to the locker room so he could grab his bag. We passed a few guys on our way whom I assumed were teammates because they greeted Freddie with a nod or pat on the back or a "We're gonna kick Manchester's arse, Saturday." A few stopped and asked Freddie for an introduction.

My cheeks warmed as I became the topic at hand. Freddie introduced me as Alice. Simple and uncomplicated.

"So, Alice," the player named Tommy said. "How did you like your backstage tour?" He and his two teammates were dressed similarly to Freddie, athletic pants and a hoodie or zip-up jacket. A typical post-workout outfit, I assumed.

"Oh, it was everything I dreamed it would be and more. The tubs for the ice baths, particularly, look so inviting. I'm thinking about getting a candle and maybe some bubble bath soap for Freddie for Christmas."

Wes, the player with blonde hair, winked. "Ah, I knew all it was missing was a woman's touch. Something to make the dreaded minutes in that frigid thing pass by."

The third guy, Nase, hit him on the back. "Toughen up, mate. You're making us look like wimps in front of the lady."

I laughed. "No way. I don't even understand how you can play outside in the cold without freezing your arses off. I just don't get the appeal. But I admire the deep dedication to your sport."

They all laughed. "Not a football fan, eh?" Tommy asked.

"Not until I met Freddie here," I replied, being honest.

"Wow, Carter," Nase said, using Freddie's last name, "how did you manage to beguile this one? It can't be your charming personality."

Freddie glared back at him, feigning a stoic face as best he could.

"Oh, Freddie knows how to captivate a woman," I said, trying to give the guy some credit. Instead, the daggers shooting from his eyes now focused on me before filling with a questioning intrigue over what exactly my words meant.

His three friends laughed, wiggling their eyebrows and patting him on the back.

"That's not…" I protested, "what I mean!" The end of that sentence more or less came out as a mumble to myself. The good-natured ribbing between teammates was unavoidable.

"Alice, it was a pleasure meeting you. Please come to a match soon. We would love to have a woman cheer for Freddie besides his sisters and mum," Wes said.

"Yeah, yeah. At least I *have* a cheering section, Wes." Freddie slapped the banter back at his friend playfully. The five of us chatted together for a few more easy minutes before they shared a half-hug, pat on the back type of thing men did when saying goodbye.

I flashed the guys a big cheeky smile as they turned to leave. "Nice to meet you guys. Don't worry; I'll be sure to cheer for you all when I make it to my first game."

"First game?" Nase called out with a whistle of amusement as they wandered away. "Freddie, mate, you need to set this girl straight right away. We'll be looking for you in the stands, Alice." He gave a friendly wink as they walked away.

Soon, we were sitting in Freddie's sportscar, heading toward the city center, with the heater on full blast and cheesy holiday tunes coming from the speakers. Freddie shot me some curious looks as I twisted the knob around, looking for the right music for a chilly winter's night. But he didn't say a word when I stopped on a station playing holiday hits. With a shrug of his shoulders, he leaned over and turned the volume up. "If we're going to celebrate the season, better go all in," he said.

I smiled at him, feeling all warm and toasty on the inside, and it wasn't just from the defrosters. A hum of genuine happiness escaped my lips. Everything was glowing and shimmering outside the car windows. Wreaths and fake snowflakes hung from city signs decked out in lights of red, green, and gold. The night held a feeling of enchantment.

Freddie had changed his clothes before he left the locker room and was wearing a soft brown sweater with a tan scarf tucked into a short jacket. He looked delicious. I couldn't help but do a double take when he casually whipped his shirt off in front of me. His back was to me, and although I couldn't report back to Emilia on the status of his six-pack, I could confirm that the man was ripped. The muscles in his back left indents up and down, like tight coils on leather. And when he stripped down to his knickers to change into jeans, good Lord, I think I might have died and gone to heaven.

For a moment, with the whimsical conditions out the car window and the devastatingly handsome man sitting next to me, I was feeling pretty damn good. So why I decided to address the elephant in the room is beyond me.

"Freddie, I feel a little silly that I had no idea you were a football star. You must think I'm dense."

He looked over at me with his forearm resting on the steering wheel, and his sexy stare burned a path of fire down my torso. "Nah, that's why I like spending time with you. You don't treat me differently. I hope that won't change."

"Ha. You're quite the lucky guy because, as far as athletic fandom goes, I could give two shites. Don't get me wrong, I will, of course, be purchasing a Chelsea jersey and rooting for you and your mates, but beyond that, you're just Freddie, the history nerd to me."

"Don't buy one," he answered.

"Why not? I know you like our…" I paused, searching for the right word. "Easy friendship, but I can't pretend that I don't know you're a football player now. That would be weird."

"No, I mean, don't buy one. I'll get you one for free." He said it all matter-of-fact like it was no big deal, but it meant he wanted me to stick around. Whatever we had going on wasn't temporary to him. He wanted me to wear his name across my chest. My cheeks bubbled up into a smile despite my failed attempts to keep it at bay.

"Will you sign it?"

"If you want me to," he replied coyly.

"What are the rules involved with this "free" jersey? Do I have to wear it around London or just at games?"

"Well, that's totally up to you."

"Can I wear it to bed? I feel like those athletic jerseys have a nice, cool feel to them. Perfect for warm nights." Sometimes, the heater in my flat malfunctioned, and I couldn't get it to turn off. In the past, Rian would fix it, but since he's been gone, it's been temperamental, and sometimes I swear I was going through early menopause.

He smirked at me, eyebrows raised in a teasing way. "I guess if that's your thing."

"Oh, my God. Are you picturing me in just your jersey and knickers?" I swatted his arm. "You're bad."

"You're the one who roused the image in my head. Not my fault. But you know, a signed jersey would probably go for a lot of money, so maybe don't wear it to bed."

"I guess you're right. Naked it is, then."

He choked at my reply, trying to play it off as a cough. I might be coming off a little forward, but that just meant I was getting my groove back. Good flirty Alice. Never knowing when to keep her snarky comments in her head.

After circling a few times, Freddie found a spot on the side of the street and parked the car. We decided to go ice skating and wander around Hyde Park, which was trimmed with every type of holiday decoration one could imagine. It was the annual Winter Wonderland Festival, and the entire park was filled with market stalls, food samples, and runway rides. We settled on a drink first to warm ourselves and ended up side by side on a bench, drinking boozy hot chocolate and careful not to let our thighs meet. *A propane-fueled log fire. Twinkling lights. Christmas wreaths. Frosted Christmas trees. Everything you could think of to create a cozy, magical atmosphere. It would be perfect for a first date. But that's not what this was, right?*

After my conversation with Scarlett, I began to feel a sort of peace within myself. She was right. Even though the heartache hurt, Rian and I had some wonderful moments together, and I couldn't just banish them from my memory. He wasn't a bad guy, no matter what I told myself while healing from the breakup. I felt like I was finally coming to terms with being on my own again. I mean, I *was* a pretty sensational human being. If I couldn't be satisfied with being single, then what luck did I have being happy with someone else? Whether or not this was really a date shouldn't matter. At least, that's what I told myself.

The impending nightfall cast shadows across Freddie's face, making the angles of his chiseled face even more defined. Once again, I wondered how I could feel so comfortable next to someone I just met a few weeks ago. Usually, I talk and talk, and people wonder when I'm going to shut up. But with Freddie, we constantly fell into moments of comfortable silence, and it was a new feeling for me. It was warm and fulfilling, like that first bite of your nan's special waffle recipe that no one else could replicate or crawling into your bed after a draining day of adulting. It was… nice. I couldn't deny that I enjoyed his company.

"This hot chocolate is glorious." The velvety milk passed my lips and settled pleasantly in my stomach, making my fingertips tingle from the alcohol.

His tongue slowly rolled across his bottom lip, tasting the whipped cream that had settled there. How I wished I was that whipped cream. "It is. Have you been here before during the holiday season?"

I nodded. "Who hasn't, right? It's such a magical place. I need your niece, Liddy, here to take notes for Saturday's Christmas market."

"She would love that. It sounds like it will be a great event. I really hope it works out for your parents. I'm sorry I can't be there."

I nodded my head as a revelation suddenly hit me. "It all makes sense now. You have a game on Saturday. That's why you can't come to the festival."

"Yeah, otherwise I would be there to help support your family. How are you handling it all? Are all the plans set in motion and ready to go?"

"Truthfully, I am a few steps from having a nervous breakdown. I want to do this for my parents, and I don't want to let them down. They don't accept help easily, and I know this has been a huge undertaking for them. And it's my home, you know? I can't lose it." Tears began to gather in the corners of my eyes, and I quickly flicked them away, forcing enthusiasm into my voice. "Sorry, I don't mean to get all sappy on you. It's just been a difficult month, but damn, this hot chocolate makes it better."

"You never have to apologize to me, Alice. I know how important family is. That's why I've been in and out of Berkingsley. My mum had hip surgery a few weeks ago, and since my dad passed away a few years ago, it falls on my sisters' and my shoulders to care for her. And being the guy in the family, the pressure falls extra hard because I feel like I have to make sure everyone is okay."

"I get it. You're the glue."

"Yeah, I'm the glue. I mean, I know it's not true. My sisters do so much for the family, and God knows no one could knock Mum down. She's made of steel and tough as a nail. She was raised on a farm with five older brothers, and my grandad made sure she bloody knew how to take care of the cattle and herself. But, still, that evolutionary male trait of needing to provide is hard to extinguish, no matter how chauvinistic it may be."

"It's clear your niece adores you, and your older sister, Sophie, seems to think you're alright." I giggled. "So, I'd say you're right where you need to be."

"Thank you." He hooked his hand around his neck, giving off the impression that he wanted to say more. But his hesitation turned to silence. We tossed our empty cups in a nearby garbage bin and decided to wander the park for a bit.

We slowly browsed the rows of items for purchase: candles that came in scents like evergreen and white Christmas, boxes of chocolate truffles tied up with little red bows, and knitted blankets in a rainbow of colors. Inside a large tent filled with displays of jewelry and clothing, a rack of winter caps caught my attention. I skipped ahead and grabbed a Santa hat and placed it on Freddie's head, removing the beanie he was wearing first. He smirked, that stoic eyebrow lifting again at me in amusement.

"Yup. I'm getting this for you, and I expect you to wear this next time you visit the bookshop. Then I'll have reassurance that you'll stop with my Christmas nickname, or you'll get your own."

"Ah, come on. You make a cute little elf. I make a pretty ugly Santa. This doesn't seem like a fair setup."

"Well, we can add the jumper if you want to increase the cuteness factor." I hold up a wool sweater with the outline of Santa's jacket stitched across the belly. "Hmm... A bit too big. I don't think they have your size." I shrugged my shoulders. "We could always stuff your shirt. It would make it more realistic, too."

I swiped the hat off his head and fake turned toward the till to pay for the items, knowing full well I would never get him into the sweater.

With a playful sigh, he grabbed the hat from my hands and placed it on his head. "Fine, you evil little elf. I'll play Santa, but I will go no further than the hat."

I pinched my lips together, stifling my grin as best I could. "Okay, but you have to wear it tonight as a test run."

He let out a *hmph* followed by an *okay*.

As we walked in the direction of the skating rink, he huffed, "God, Alice. Does everyone always follow along with your plans, or am I just a sucker?"

"That's a very serious question, Freddie Carter. I'd have to say... a little of both.

"Are you ready to ice skate?"

"I was born to ice skate."

Fifteen minutes later, my fingers clutched Freddie's arm as I shuffled clumsily along the ice like a newborn deer learning to use her legs. A round later, I realized that the notion of ice skating might have played out more romantically in my head. Turns out, I was not born to ice skate.

"I might have exaggerated a bit when I proclaimed my ice-skating abilities. How about we throw in the towel and finish our night with a spin around that?" I lifted my chin to the night sky.

Freddie's eyes widened in amazement as we both looked up at the giant observation wheel that spanned the skyline. I grabbed his hand and pulled him over to the ticket booth.

A few minutes later, we were sitting in our private pod, making our way slowly around the globe, abruptly stopping every minute or so as groups of people entered the queue. As we reached the top, I sucked in a quick, frosty breath as I took in the scene before me. The view was spectacular. Amongst the treetops, strung glimmers of lights in every color. Children waved glow sticks, and couples walked hand in hand like miniature figurines in a dollhouse. I pulled out my mobile, wanting to take a photo of the sweeping view. I grabbed a few shots and turned to snap one of Freddie, but his face was buried between his legs.

"What are you doing? You're missing the sights, silly."

He lifted his head, and all I could think was that he was far from photo-ready. I lowered my phone. "You look like you're about to vomit. Are you okay?" I asked, suddenly concerned.

"Yeah. I'm just a bit afraid of heights. I'll be alright."

"Oh blimey, Freddie! Why did you let me drag you on here?"

"I told you; I can't say no to you. Plus, you looked positively jubilant when you mentioned it. I'll be okay. It's just a few minutes more, right?"

"Well, seeing how we haven't even finished our first 360-degree rotation, it might be more like ten."

"Oh, God." He looked positively sick.

I dug through my purse and pulled out a pack of Tic Tacs. I shook them in relief. "Here, hold out your hand. These will help."

"Tic Tacs? Really?"

"Trust me. This will work." I poured a few into his hands. "Suck on them, don't chew. And under your tongue, sir." I saw his tongue move in his mouth. I turned his face toward mine. "Good. Now, just look at me and not beyond. Tell me, what did you get your sweet niece for Christmas?"

I distracted Freddie with small talk until we finally reached the bottom, and the wheel stopped. As we found our feet back firmly on the ground, I linked my arm through Freddie's. "If only your friends knew that the strong, brave football man is afraid of a child's ride."

He feigned a look of shock and clutched his chest. "You wouldn't."

"I'm just teasing. Pinky promise. But it's just because you're still wearing the Santa hat."

"Well, I owe my survival to you. Those Tic Tacs were a lifesaver. I hadn't realized they helped with acrophobia."

"Me either. They were the only things I could find in my purse that could serve as a distraction. I'm glad it worked."

He clapped his hands together as he chuckled. "Oh, Alice. You're really something."

"Well, thank you." I was beginning to think so, too, again.

We drove back to Berkingsley in a comfortable silence, both of us lost in thought. Mine immediately landed on this thing Freddie and I had going on. The fastest way to get over someone was to get under someone. That's the advice I usually gave my friends after a breakup. But something about this time felt different. Maybe it's because I'm not twenty-two anymore. Maybe it's because I was now well aware of what it felt like to get my heart broken, and I didn't want to risk that happening again. I knew that I had to take whatever this was with Freddie slowly.

He pulled up to the entrance and hopped out of the car, opening the door for me and offering a strong hand. "Thanks for a great night, Alice. Let me know how the Christmas market goes on Saturday."

Before I gave him the opportunity for more, I planted a quick peck on his cheek and scampered away. "Thanks, Freddie. I had a lovely time as well. Good luck at your game."

"Match."

"What?" I asked, turning back.

"It's called a match," he said with a sly smile.

I giggled. "Right. Good luck at your match."

I gave a slight wave from the doorway, watching him return to his car, and smiled at myself. It had been a long time since I had a night as fun as this one.

CHAPTER 11

Let There Be Peace on Earth
(and in Berkingsley)

When Saturday morning came around, all the nervous energy that had been building all week left me feeling like the main character from *Frozen*. The pressure from our money-raising efforts felt almost as big as coronation day. When my alarm chimed, I jumped out of bed, the adrenaline already running through my veins. The market didn't open until 11 a.m., but we needed a few hours to set everything up. Pippy, who had been snuggled tightly against my belly, didn't appreciate my early morning enthusiasm. She rolled over with a grumble and a yawn and nestled herself deeper into the duvet cover.

"Today is not the day to suddenly become an adolescent, Pips," I said in a singsong voice. "It's go-time in Santa Land."

As I got myself ready, the steamy romance novel I had

on audiobook played through my mobile speaker, but my mind was too anxious to pay attention. After the third replay of chapter four, I gave up and blasted my favorite hits from Taylor Swift's *Lover* album instead. Even the queen was telling me to calm down. Showered, hair blown, and dressed like the embarrassing aunt at the family holiday party, I was ready to perform a Christmas miracle. I sent a message to Emilia.

> **ME:** You ready, lady?

> **EMILIA:** So ready. Meet you at the truck in ten?

> **ME:** Perfect.

All of the supplies sat waiting at the bookshop, so I only had to prepare Pippy. I quickly dressed her in a cozy elf sweater that matched mine, and we ventured outside.

"Rise and Shine, Sleeping Beauty!" Theo greeted us as we met him at his truck.

"Good morning, dorkface," I replied lovingly. "Are you ready to sell some vino?"

"You bet! I'm hoping the weather will stay this mild all day so we'll get a good turnout. And if not, maybe people will load up on the vino to ward off the cold." He gave a good-natured laugh.

"It's kind of exciting to be a part of the festival, isn't it?" I asked, hopping in the truck. "Usually, we just spectate or come late for the bonfire."

"There's a bonfire?" Emilia asked from the backseat of the truck.

"Oh, it's quite the spectacle. After the market closes around 4 p.m., all the older folks of the village go back to their comfortable houses and the festivities turn over to the young people. There's music, drinking, and roasting of spider dogs and marshmallows. As long as they clean up their mess and don't get too rowdy, the village supervisor looks the other way. It's been a village tradition for as long as I can remember."

"Unfortunately, it seems we have finally reached the old folk status. Here we are, participating in the festival instead of the twilight activities. Feels a bit like we should be mourning," I said melodramatically.

"We're about five years past our prime, Alice. I think last time the kids thought we were chaperones trying to break up the fun."

"The kids…" Emilia repeated, grinning from ear to ear. "Yeah, I'd say you're better off running the festival these days, babe."

He wiggled his eyebrows at her in the rearview mirror. "I stopped playing drinking games when I met you, love. Now, I can't wait to settle down, get married, and spend all my nights in bed with you."

"Ew. Stop. Gross." I said, putting my fingers in my ears. Theo pulled up to Spines 'n' Wines, and we unloaded the speaker Trevor had on loan from The Royal Albert Music Hall. A few of Emilia's students agreed to serenade us on the keyboard with Christmas tunes throughout the day, but during the times they were on break, we wanted to make

sure we had festive music playing to catch the attention
of people walking by the shop.

Early yesterday evening, Theo and my dad had assembled the tent in front of the store. The three main roads on
this block of the village had been shut down for the day's
festivities, so there was plenty of space. Many businesses
on the road had their own tents up, and there was also
a central area where individual vendors could sell their
goods. Two long gray tables sat parallel underneath our tent,
and a square table stood in the back corner. It all looked
a little drab. Emilia shook her head, staring at the setup.

"Are you thinking what I'm thinking?"

"It's a good thing we got here early, right?"

"Right. Let's put our creative minds to work," she said.

We spent the next hour laying out red and green pol-
ka-dotted tablecloths and wrapping the poles of the tent
with green garland that shimmered with gold LED lights.
Theo headed to the eatery, making sure everything was
set for the wine-tasting booth with Scarlett, but before he
left, he secured the speakers to the base of the tent legs
and connected them to the keyboard. Emilia and I danced
playfully around the tent to a pop Christmas playlist that
played through the speakers as we decorated. With just an
hour to go before the festival began, we filled bowl after
bowl with assortments of candy and icing for gingerbread
house decorating. The square table held a clipboard with
a sign-up list for the contest that would follow and a cash
box for donations in case people didn't want to give elec-
tronically. We also had boxes and boxes of graham crackers
and gingerbread stacked in piles, ready for construction.

As a last-minute surprise, yesterday, Freddie's sister had dropped off a painted sign to the store that read, "Gingerbread House Contest." Each red letter was meticulously outlined in green glitter paint, courtesy of Liddy's creative eye. A caption underneath stated that all donations for supplies would go directly toward keeping the bookstore open. Propped on a stand, it was the perfect addition to the front of the tent. Tomorrow, we were going to hold a festive party at Blackley Manor where people could cast their votes on which Gingerbread House they favored the most.

After we added the finishing touches, we stepped onto the cobblestone street to admire our work. The nervous energy in my stomach dissolved instantly as I gazed upon our festive setup. It was a good thing I loved Christmas because all of this decorating really was making me feel like I had picked up a second job as an elf.

"I think it looks beautiful, Alice. It really came together."

I linked arms with Em and gave her a squeeze. "Thank you, love. I agree. Oh," I said, unlinking my arm and walking behind the square table to grab a stack of green and red construction paper from my bag. "I almost forgot these. In case you want to share your countdown tradition with the kids. I also brought tape and scissors."

Emilia's eyes grew damp. "Oh, Alice. Thank you. Thank you for including my mom in the day."

I took her hand in mine and squeezed it. "Well, without her, you wouldn't be in Berkingsley, and I would be without my best friend. I'd be honored if you shared her tradition with others in the village."

Before we could get too weepy, Mum and Dad walked out the front door of the shop, breaking up the moment. I had asked them to stay inside until the festival started, tasking Dad with keeping an eye on Pippy. They still felt uncomfortable accepting help from the community, so I was trying to involve them in the details as little as possible. This was my gift to them, and I didn't want them worrying about anything.

Mum pulled me into a soft hug. "Alice, this is so wonderful. Thank you for doing all this for us."

"Of course, Mum. I'd do anything for you and Dad. The bookstore is not just home to us; it belongs to everyone in the village."

My dad gave me a side squeeze. "We're so proud of you, Alice dear. Sometimes I forget that you aren't my little girl anymore. You are a trailblazer, and it makes me so happy to see you doing what you do best, leading and taking care of others."

"It's nothing. Really. I love you both. Now, head on inside and get prepared for the customers we send your way. Scoot!"

Groups of people started to gather and wander around the village center, bundled up in scarves, hats, and gloves, filtering in and out of the tents lined up on the road. The day was pretty mild except for a slight breeze that would come and go, adding a bitter chill when it did. But along with the snap of cold, it also brought a whiff of roasted chestnuts and the sweet scent of cinnamon-coated almonds. So, I didn't mind the wind. Emilia's students filtered through in shifts every thirty minutes, some playing classical Christmas songs, others a playlist of jazzy renditions, and one animated teenager even drew the crowd into a sing-along.

Emilia and I took turns outside the tent, one of us encouraging passing spectators to design a gingerbread house while the other helped inside with contest registration and refilling supplies. Turn-out was slow at first, but once a few groups of people began decorating, others became interested in what they were doing. Soon, both tables were at full capacity, and I found myself walking in circles, refilling the candy bowls, registering people, and answering any questions people might have.

The wind picked up after a bit, and the warm sweat that had formed underneath my winter jacket started to give me a chill. But I was so chuffed at how things were going that I barely gave it a second thought. At one point, I looked across the tent at Em and gave her a huge grin. She returned my smile with one of her own and a thumbs up. We were doing this. We were going to save my parents' bookshop. I just knew it.

The jingling bells of a sleigh suddenly became audible over the energized voices of the young children and competitive teenagers building their creations. I looked up at the sound of a horse whinnying and saw Trevor and Noah at the front of a three-row horse-driven sleigh. Noah played the part of refined coachman, in a black formal jacket and a tall top hat. Trevor, on the other hand, with his cheeks and nose glowing almost as bright as his ginger hair, looked absolutely miserable. He sat rigid as a soldier on top of the black seat cushion, his head buried within his shoulders, holding a paper cup in each hand.

I hurried over and shouted up at them, "I can't believe you're driving that thing." Noah had negotiated a tough sale for one of his property clients, who happened to be a friend, and as a thank-you, the man had allowed him to borrow his horse and sleigh for the day. The money raised from the sleigh rides would be going straight to my parents' shop.

"Hey, I look pretty good on top of here, don't I? Maybe I'll take up a new hobby."

"No freakin' way. You're on your own then," Trevor answered. He leaned over in my direction and attempted a strained smile that looked more like he was in pain than enjoying the festivities. "Alice, I've got a delivery for you and Emilia. One hot chocolate and one caramel latte with extra whip, courtesy of Theo."

"Oh, wow. That's great. Thanks, Trevor." I took both covered cups from his hands and embraced the heat that radiated from the cardboard. "The magic is already working. Tell Theo thanks as well." I took a sip from the hot chocolate. The rich liquid warmed my insides instantly. Delicious.

"How are the rides going? Are you getting many passengers?"

"Yes, we've been doing rides back-to-back since 11 a.m. Just took a quick detour to deliver these goodies to you. Looks like you've been pretty busy too!"

"I'm so glad to hear that, and yes, we have! I have a good feeling about this, guys. Thank you again for all of your help today."

Noah bowed his head with a salute, "Of course, my lady. Anything for a friend. We'd better get back before our line of customers get too anxious. Ta-ta." He tipped his hat at me, and I curtseyed back. What happy idiots we were. Gosh, I was enjoying this too much.

Before returning to the tent, I took a peek at my mobile to check the score of the "football match." They were sixty minutes in, and it looked like Freddie had scored again. It seemed that he was having a good afternoon as well. Seeing his name on the screen warmed me up even more than the hot chocolate. I couldn't wait to congratulate him later. *Look at me, caring about sports for the first time in my life.* My dad was going to be overjoyed by this new development. He'd always wanted a sidekick when he watched football on the telly.

Emilia nudged me, taking hold of her latte and motioning me to switch places. I took up the task of greeting everyone and explaining the details of the contest. The wind continued to blow, and it suddenly felt like the temperature was taking a nosedive. All the hot chocolate and scored goals in the world couldn't keep me warm anymore if this kept up. I suppose I should have worn real trousers instead of the polka dot red and green stockings I sported. But where was the fun in that? Freddie was right. Deep down, I was made to be Santa's little helper. I pulled my scarf tighter around my neck, and out of the corner of my eye, I saw a little brown-haired girl with purple earmuffs scurrying over to me.

"Hi, Alice! You hung up our sign!"

"Of course I did! Hi Liddy. It was so thoughtful of you and your mum to paint it for us."

"My mum is really talented at drawing, and I like to paint. Uncle Freddie mentioned that you might need a sign, so we made it together during our craft time. I'm so glad you fancy it because Andrew stepped on it before it was dry, and we had to redo that part." She wrinkled her nose in annoyance.

"I hadn't even noticed. It's perfect. Where's your mum now?"

She turned and pointed behind her. Sophie was talking to a woman but noticed Liddy pointing, so she gave a quick wave. "Where is your little brother?"

"He stayed home with Dad. We thought he'd complain too much, so we made it a girl's day out! They're watching Uncle Freddie play football on the telly. Can I help decorate a gingerbread house?"

"You sure can! I'll get you started, and then you and your mum can work together."

I gathered a bowl of graham crackers for her and found an empty place at the table. There were many empty places now. Only one other family remained, and Emilia was currently carrying their decorated house into the bookshop for safekeeping until the contest the next day. I glanced at the time and noticed it was only a little past two o'clock. The tablecloths had started flapping around, and a cold drizzle began to patter off the tent roof. Sophie, holding her purse over her head, jogged over to the tent.

"Brr. What a sopping mess this weather has become! How are you, Alice?"

"Hi, Sophie. It's so good to see you and Liddy. Thank you again for your gracious donation of the sign for our event. It was a splendid way to bring people into our tent! I know it doesn't look like it, but we've been quite busy in the last three hours. It just began to clear out."

"Yeah, it looked like a lot of people were leaving when we started walking this way. It's only supposed to get colder and wetter in the next hour."

"Oh, gross. Those aren't the best conditions for outdoor activities." As the words left my mouth, the collection of plastic knives and bowls of candy blew off the tables and onto the ground. Sophie and I rushed to grab them before they propelled down the cobblestone road. Emilia exited the bookshop in a flurry to help. After we collected the cutlery that blew away, she told us that the festival was slowing down at the other end of the road, according to a text from Theo.

"Oh blimey, this doesn't sound good at all."

"Maybe it will pass," Emilia said in a hopeful voice.

"Doesn't sound like it, according to the weather update on my phone," Sophie said. "Why don't Liddy and I help you move everything inside and maybe people who are left will venture in to warm up?"

"Fabulous idea," I said. "Let me get a marker. Liddy, is it okay if we add *Come Inside* to the bottom of your sign?"

Her lips pinched together as she gave it some thought. "Oh definitely, Miss Alice. I think that would be a rather smart idea."

Together, the four of us, joined by my mum and dad, carried all the supplies inside within a few minutes, starting with the keyboard and speakers.

"I guess now we wait and see," I mumbled under my breath.

The crappy weather sent everyone scurrying back to their dry, warm homes, and that eventually included me. I wasn't one to mope or feel sorry for myself when things went wrong, but this was bigger than myself. All I could think about was Mummy's comforting smile, growing warm from the oven steam as she baked our favorite casserole, and Dad clapping his hands together, reporting the daily bookshop sales while we spooned chicken and biscuits into our mouths. Images flashed in my mind of Scarlett and me transforming into our childhood selves, fighting over who would get the first bite of the chocolate cream pie when we came home to visit. Spines 'n' Wines was our home and after the poor afternoon turnout this morning, it looked like it would only be ours for a short time longer.

In my ultimate state of self-pity, I stupidly picked up my mobile and rolled my thumbs over the screen until I found Rian's Instagram page. I was already feeling low. Why not dig myself deeper into the pit of desolation? I was getting good at playing the victim card. Somewhere deep in my head, I knew clicking on @Hot_(r)AF_Dude was a completely idiotic thing to do. He'd kept the username I created for him as a prank last summer, and even though I now saw that as a screaming sign of his minuscule level of maturity, at the time, my lovesick heart only carried warm and fuzzy feelings. Now it flashed at me like a neon sign at the pub. How could I have missed the warnings?

My thumb hovered above his feed, about to start scrolling down out of habit, careful not to double tap, when I stopped myself. Did I really care what Rian was doing or what girl he might be seeing? I didn't, I realized. I gave zero shites what was going on in that man's life anymore. Even though the weight of the day's failed events held me down, a part of me felt so much lighter without the heartache there.

Nestled under the covers and half a bottle of red wine later, I had finally allowed my brain to rest. My imagination ran wild as I dived back into the steamy cowboy romance I had on audiobook. Clara was about to get her boots knocked off her by the hunky ranch hand when my mobile buzzed, and a text bubble popped on screen. There appeared two simple words that held such possibility, especially after the sex scene I had just devoured.

> **FREDDIE (HOT FOOTBALL GUY):** Hey you.

Where did I go from here? Did I answer honestly and include him in my doom and gloom? Or did I put the focus on his amazing win on the football field? Or did I simply respond...

> **ME:** Hey.

> **FREDDIE (HOT FOOTBALL GUY):** What are you doing?

> **ME:** Hmm... well. I'm currently lying in bed, with a glass of red wine and a book. I saw that you had a great match today. I'm so happy for you and the guys.

FREDDIE (HOT FOOTBALL GUY): Thanks, Alice. We're pretty chuffed with the turnout. Can I video call you?

Before I could give him an answer, his image popped up on my screen. I watched as his hand raked through his short hair as he waited for me to answer. I fluffed out my own hair and sat up a bit straightener against the frame of the hotel bed. Then I pushed 'accept.'

His mouth broadened into a smile when he saw me. Even in my despondent state, his grin stirred feelings of excitement down in my belly.

"I just wanted to see what you were wearing," he said.

"Woah, you get right to the point, don't you?"

"I needed to see how urgent your request was for this jersey. And the verdict is in. There's no rush. Those pajamas suit you just fine."

I looked down at the tiny pink tank top I was wearing, paired with a pair of lacy white shorts that barely covered the top of my thighs. My eyes shrank at him. "Just fine, huh?"

"I was trying my best to be gentlemanly. What I mean is that they're hot. You look hot. I mean, not literally hot. I think you're probably quite cold wearing those in winter. But then again, I sleep naked. So, who am I to judge?"

"Oh my gosh, Freddie! I didn't think you had it in you to nervous-ramble. You must be spending entirely too much time with me." I frowned at my statement.

"Oh, is that not a good thing?"

"No, that's not it. I'm just thinking that it's been a few days since we hung out, and I kind of miss you." I froze for a moment. What was I doing?

He grinned so big that the ridged dimple along his mouth made an appearance, and I immediately felt at ease. "I kind of miss you too, Alice. You were on my mind all day. How did the Christmas Festival go?"

"Not that well. The weather took a turn for the worst, and the crowds died pretty early. With a little over twenty entries for tomorrow's contest, I don't think we will make enough in ticket sales to come close to the numbers we need to keep the shop afloat."

"Sophie told me that the afternoon crowd was sparse. I hadn't realized just how much it would affect your overall efforts. I'm so sorry, Alice. I know how much you depended on this to be successful."

"Yeah, it sucks. I feel like I've let my parents down. They had accepted the fate of the shop, and I had to wedge my zealous ideas into the mix. Overly confident, know-it-all Alice, mucking it all up for everyone."

"You mean to say, compassionate and resolute. You saw your family hurting and you took action. That's admirable, Alice. Give yourself some credit." He grew quiet for a moment, twisting his lips in thought. "I have an idea. Give me an hour to work some things out. We might just be able to get that Christmas miracle."

"What do you mean, Freddie?"

"Just—give me an hour. We're not giving up that easily."

His screen turned black, leaving me alone in the hotel room wondering what plan he could possibly be plotting, and stuck on the fact that he called us a 'we.'

CHAPTER 12

White Christmas
(Just like in Boston)

"Holy shite, Alice. I still can't believe you neglected to tell us that your new boyfriend is Freddie Carter from the Chelsea Football team. What the hell, woman? That is not something you hold back from your friends." Noah's football commentary had been going non-stop for the last hour while he and Trevor unloaded the gingerbread displays from Theo's truck into the foyer of Blackley Manor. Tables, covered in shimmery white cloth, had been set up in a sort of half square in the open area of the room. It was a day late, but the sun shone through the long front windows as if it was showing off its tan, casting light across the marble floor and following it up the intricately curved staircase. It was the day of the Gingerbread Contest, and we were just about done setting up.

"For the tenth time, Noah, he is **not** my boyfriend!" I shouted across the room.

"Just keep your focus, boys. Last one to go." My sister's glasses slid down her nose as she double-checked the to-do list on her tablet. Scarlett did not take her job as hotel operations manager lightly on a day-to-day basis. Throw in an event that had so much at stake; well, let's just say her inner boss girl was showing up in two-inch gold stilettos. "Turn that last display a bit so it faces the door. Perfect."

Theo kept the conversation going as he added across the room, "*I* can't believe you didn't recognize Freddie Carter. He's like the only famous person that has come out of Berkingsley. How did you not know that, Alice?"

I rolled my eyes at him. "Seriously? I couldn't even name one football team before last week. You really think I'd care about a local player? It's not like he was in my school year. If he graduated before you, he's at least five years older than me!"

"Yeah, he was one year ahead of me and Scarlett. But geez, everyone in the village knows about Freddie."

"Well, clearly not everyone," I muttered back.

"People. Stop the yapping and get back to work. We all know Alice wasn't particularly keen on sports growing up. But I'm sure that will all change soon enough," my sister said with a smug grin.

"Yes, I suppose it will," I said, lifting my eyebrows at her mischievously.

"What's most important here is that we are sure to get some VIP perks now that our girl, here, is dating the star player of the team," Noah said, straightening the last table and then brushing his hands together.

"Again, Noah. He is **not** my boyfriend." I shook my head at the obnoxious commentary that was now starting to give me a headache.

I tried to focus on the sweet scents of cinnamon, sugar, and vanilla that floated up from the tables, making the hotel entrance smell like a childhood dream. Two dozen buildings constructed from graham crackers sat in a row, thankfully all still intact due to Scarlett's watchful eye. There was no limit to the creativity of the entries. One display looked like a board game of Candy Land, with 3D replicas of Peppermint Forest, Gumdrop Mountain, and King Kandy's castle. It was quite detailed, but was the concept creative enough? Debatable. My favorite was the recreation of Spines 'n" Wines, complete with chocolate bar bookshelves and grumpy little Winston molded from a lump of frosting. The winner of the contest was not up to me, though. The $100 gift certificate to Mae's Eatery, a bottle of wine, and a free weekend stay at Blackley Manor went to the display that received the most votes from today's guests. Of course, if a child won, the award converted to a shopping spree at the local toy store and a monthly box of assorted cookies from William's bakery.

"Hey, Alliecakes," Scarlett shouted across the room at me, using the nickname she christened me with as a child. I couldn't fault her for the name; my obsession with Victoria Sponge Cakes led to an annual birthday cake made of whipped cream and jam. My mouth watered every time she used the nickname.

"Yes, big sis?" I shouted back from the dining room without looking up. My focus was on the little vases that

I was arranging, filling each glass with a spring of holly and a stem of baby's breath.

"Let Theo know that the bags of ice are out in the boot of my motor."

"Will do. Did you hear that, Theo?" I shouted toward the bar where I had last seen him mixing up a special fruity concoction he was calling *Milia's Christmas Punch* and a batch of spiked hot chocolate for the adults. Emilia was behind the bar filling plates with buttery shortbread cookies that William undoubtedly baked at 4 a.m. this morning. The dear old man had hired help last year for his business, but he still insisted on personally having his hands in the dough for events or people that were special to him.

"Theo's in the back grabbing some marshmallows, but I'll let him know," Emilia called back. If this day had a happy ending, we really should consider running a private cruise ship. We all worked together like the hospitality crew on David Beckham's private yacht. Damn, if only I could find a job where I could see David Beckham shirtless…

"Hey, there." A sexy male voice pulled me right out of my daydreams, but when I turned around, I irrevocably found myself plopped into a real-life fantasy. Right there in front of me stood the most attractive man I ever laid eyes on. Strong symmetrical face, a shadow of facial hair encompassing a wide, gorgeous smile. White dress shirt. Black trousers. Black suspenders and a tight silver chain around his neck. Blimey, I think I might have peed myself a little.

"Freddie," I said, flustered. The fuzzy feeling floating around in my head left me void of words.

"I have an important question only the boss can answer. Hat," he said, holding up the Santa hat we purchased from the festival, "or no hat."

The teasing look in his eyes brought me back to reality. "Oh, come on. Is that even a real question? Hat. 100 hundred percent," I said, taking it from his hands and placing it on his head.

As I adjusted the end of it, he grabbed my hand to stop me. The playful glimmer in his eyes turned to the smokey intensity they often held. Our faces were inches away from each other, and though we were alone in the corner of the dining room, I'm sure all my friends were pretending not to watch our interaction from afar.

"I'm sorry I couldn't get out here yesterday. I really wish I was there for you." He brought my hand to his side but didn't let go.

My lungs took a quick breath, holding it captive, and I felt an endless warmth engulf every part of me. My eyes searched his for a brief moment, wondering what meaning his words held. This man, God, he did something to me. How did he make me feel so vibrant and alive one moment and so safe and secure the next?

"I know," I managed to murmur. "But I'm okay now. Talking to you last night helped more than you know. And I can't thank you enough for all that you did to make today work. You've pretty much reached hero status in my eyes." After our conversation yesterday, Freddie called in a favor from some of his teammates. He and his two friends, Tommy and Wes, would be serving drinks behind the bar today. A simple post on his social media page sharing the news had our event sold out within the hour! Looks like I wasn't the only person excited to see this man.

"Alice, I told you, I can't say no to you. I'd do anything to see you smile. Besides, my mates owed me a favor after I saved their arses from the paps. Photos of them half naked on the lions at Trafalgar Square would not have gone over well with the PR team."

"Seriously?" My lips formed a smile mere inches away from his face. I could feel the minty warmth of his breath mixed with mine.

"Oh yeah. It's quite the story." He leaned closer and his voice grew husky. "But right now, I wanted to tell you—"

Before he could finish his sentence, Noah's voice cut through the room, abruptly extinguishing the intoxicating moment. We stepped apart awkwardly, and Freddie ran his hands over his head as Noah approached us. Excitement was radiating from every pore of his body, from his wide eyes to the giddy smile on his face. He clapped his hands together and brought one to his mouth, biting his fist. "Oh man, Freddie Carter. I can't believe I'm meeting you. How are you, man?"

"Hello, mate. You must be a friend of Alice's?"

"Yes. Yes, I am. The name's Noah."

"Hi, Noah. Thanks for doing all the heavy lifting this morning. I'm sorry I wasn't here to help."

"Oh, it was no big deal. I wasn't able to catch the match yesterday, but I followed along on my phone. Two goals. Congrats, buddy." His weight shifted side to side as his words flew out eagerly.

"Well, thank you so much, Noah."

Behind him, Trevor hustled over, breathing heavily and shaking his ginger head profusely. "Sorry for the rude interruption, Alice. Noah doesn't understand the concept of privacy or tactfulness." He shot Noah a stern look from behind his glasses that belonged to a teacher in a classroom. "Hi, I'm Trevor, Noah's boyfriend," He extended his hand to Freddie.

Freddie gave it a hefty shake in return. "Ah, it's alright guys. It's a pleasure to meet you both. I'm Freddie."

"Oh, I know all about you and your team, Freddie. Noah hasn't shut his mouth all morning," Trevor whined.

"Noah's love of the game seems to make up for my lack of enthusiasm," I added with a smirk.

"Something tells me that you'll soon have a renewed interest in the sport." Trevor winked at me.

I grinned at Freddie demurely. "Yeah, I think so too." A quick glance at my watch told me that we needed to wrap up the small talk and get ready for guests. Scarlett noticed the same thing and, of course, immediately took control. Her heels echoed off the marble floor as she demanded everyone's attention. Theo and Emilia stopped their work at the bar, and we gathered around my sister.

Scarlett flicked her thick mahogany hair back behind her shoulders. She scrolled down her tablet with a pen, getting right to business. "Alright, babes. First off, Alice and I want to thank you for all the help you've given this weekend. We know our parents are beyond grateful, no matter how this turns out. Alice?" She nodded her head in my direction, putting the spotlight on me.

"Yes, thank you so much. You all are the best friends a girl could have. It's been a difficult season for my family and, well… me, but you've all been so understanding. I can't thank you enough. I love you guys." Emilia squeezed my hand beside me. "Okay, enough with the sentiments. I told myself I would *not* cry today." Soft laughter from my friends filled the air. "Now, I need to officially tell you the best news. Thanks to Freddie and his teammates, ticket sales for the event skyrocketed overnight, and we are extremely close to reaching our goal." I hoped Freddie could see how close my heart was to bursting with gratitude. Beside me, my friends hooted and cheered. "It only took a couple of football guys dressed in their finest to get us across the finish line. So, let's get this done! We're going to save the bookstore!"

Scarlett quickly reminded everyone of their duties during the event. Armed with her tablet, she and Trevor would be checking people in at the door, ensuring everyone had a ticket, and no superfans were trying to sneak in. Theo and Emilia were tasked with maintaining the bar and making sure the food and drinks were stocked. Admission sales ended this morning and each included two drinks and five tickets for voting in the gingerbread contest. Any drinks beyond that would be an additional cost, and Theo was prepared to check IDs and collect payment.

Against Scarlett's better judgment, I insisted that Noah had free reign of the music that played through the speakers in the room. I knew he would keep it fun and festive. Freddie and his teammates were serving drinks at the bar, and I would be keeping an eye on the tables of gingerbread houses. With their instructions from Scarlett, everyone scattered to their places, ready for the crowd to filter in. Freddie's teammates, Wes and Tommy, had arrived and were behind the bar, getting directions from Freddie. I headed over to say hello and extend my gratitude for them stepping in to help.

"Tommy! Wes! I didn't know athletes could clean up so well. Thank you for giving up your Sunday afternoon to help a small-town girl save the village bookshop. Sounds like something right out of a Christmas novel."

"No problem, Alice. Any friend of Freddie's is a friend of ours," Wes said with charm.

"What he means is we owed Freddie big time from saving our arses a few weeks ago. And you seemed like a cool girl the other day, so we don't mind donating our services."

"Could have gotten a bit more if we auctioned them off for dates. There's still time. Right, mates?" Freddie elbowed Tommy in the ribs. "I know you guys need some help on the dating front. This could be the perfect opportunity."

"Oh, definitely!" I played along. "There are a few older ladies in our town who would love to have something to talk about at their next puzzle club meeting. A date with a much younger athlete? I bet that could go for a large sum of money."

Wes and Tommy grew fidgety, looking at each other like they didn't know what they had gotten themselves into. "Well, um, you know, I'm not sure that would-"

"I'm totally pulling one on ya, boys. Geez, how big is that debt you have to repay Freddie?" They both broke into nervous laughter at my question.

"Let's just say that I'm never drinking a Moscow mule ever again, even if I live to one hundred," Wes admitted. He seemed to blech at the mere thought.

Tommy handed me a bag from behind the bar. "Alice, we brought along two of Freddie's jerseys, one for you to keep and one to raffle off. That should help bring some money in."

"Oh, yeah," Wes said. "Way more than a date with us. I mean, look at the guy!" He grabbed Freddie's cheeks and squeezed them together. "Who wouldn't want a signed jersey with his name on it?"

Freddie shrugged him off. "Good save, guys. Guess we won't need to run the dating auction. I'm sure the jersey will help bring in some revenue. I heard it's getting popular amongst the ladies as a sexy nightgown." He stared me straight in the eyes, with a slight smirk on his lips as he said that last bit.

I stared right back, ignoring the confused look on his friends' faces, not intimidated by Freddie's insinuation in the least. I lifted my shoulders in defiance and licked my top lip. "Hmm, who knew?" Before we could venture into this new game of flirting, our first guests filtered through the double doors of the hotel.

"Show's starting, boys. Knock 'em dead."

I headed toward the tables, ready to mingle and greet the faces that walked by, many of whom I had known for years and others who were making their first visit to Berkingsley. I issued thank-yous and rattled off instructions on how the contest worked to people gazing upon the displays. The mood in the air was festive, enhanced by the beautiful Christmas decor throughout the first floor of the hotel and the Christmas playlist Noah was controlling from his phone. Classy golden lights strung across the ceiling, illuminating the room as the sun began its journey home for the evening. Combinations of red bows, poinsettias, and evergreens wrapped around the black bars of the elegant staircase banister, forming a Christmas garland that was as aesthetically pleasing to the eyes as it was to the nose. To top it off, a stunning eight-foot-tall Christmas pine stood at the front of the dining area, framing the tall windows and giving a show to all the people who entered.

I loved a good celebration, and even though this event was born out of an impossibly dire situation, it turned out that even joy could be found amongst the difficult things in life. I looked around at my friends who selflessly gave up their weekend to help my family, and I knew in my heart that I was lucky. Neighbors filtered in: friends of my mother who would give her the clothes off their back, the local business owners wanting to show their support for another village treasure, and the young kids excited for yet another Christmas event in town. I glanced over at my parents talking animatedly to their friends. My dad caught my eye and gave me an encouraging nod. My heart felt full, and it wasn't just because I knew my parents would be okay. It was because I knew *I'd* be okay, too. It didn't matter whether I had a man beside me or if I stood on my own two feet. I was bound for good things.

My attention shifted to Freddie and his teammates, who were serving the drinks at the bar. Between ladles of punch and hot chocolate, all three were gracefully accepting the praise bestowed upon them by beguiled fans, even offering to sign a few hats and photographs people had brought along with them. Sophie and her husband arrived with kids in tow, and I watched as Liddy immediately scampered over to Freddie, who picked her up and twirled her around in the air. Whether this thing with him and I developed into something more or remained strictly in the friend zone, I was glad that I had met a decent guy who gave me hope for future relationships. I had been in love, and my heart had been broken. But here I was, still willing to risk it all for a chance at finding that spark again.

People waltzed in and out the next two hours, placing votes for their favorite display, mingling with friends, and enjoying holiday treats as music filled the air. Elton John and Ed Sheeran were in the middle of praying for December snow when the clamor of a bell floated through the lobby. *That's not… that couldn't be… Oh blimey.*

In ran Maggie, with Pippy fresh on her heels, whining her little yip as she frantically tried to catch up to her friend. All decked out in her elf sweater with attached jingle bells, it was hard not to follow her tracks. The pair weaved in and out of the tables, causing them to wobble, and dozens of gasps filled the room. I held my breath and said a little prayer that the gingerbread men would live to see another day. When the jingle bells finished their song, I opened my eyes and said an early Happy Birthday to baby Jesus and thanked him for saving the displays from ulti-mate doom. Pippy nestled unperturbed in my dad's arms while Maggie Girl sat at Theo's feet, looking apologetically guilty. Suddenly, the Christmas carols were replaced by "Who Let the Dogs Out" by Baha Men, and the tension in the air was replaced by chuckles and clapping. Never a dull moment in my life, I swear.

After the winners of the contest and raffle were announced, the crowd dwindled, and the event eventually came to a close. Scarlett tallied up the profits from the bar and raffle, and with a toast over glasses of Christmas punch, she announced that we had done it. Our efforts were a success, and my parents' home and business would be saved.

Emilia approached me from behind, putting her chin on my shoulder. "I'm so proud of you, my dearest friend. You made all this happen. Look at how happy your mom and dad look. This will be a Christmas you'll never forget."

I turned around and hugged my best friend. "I couldn't have done it without you, Emilia. Thank you for always having my back."

"Speaking of a Christmas, you'll never forget... Milia, you need to come outside." Theo grabbed her hand and pulled her toward the hotel entrance.

"Oo, if we weren't already engaged, I would think you were about to propose," she giggled.

I followed right behind them, my curiosity piqued by Theo's excitement. Freddie, his teammates, Noah and Trevor also joined in line to see what the commotion was all about.

The winter air greeted us with a blustery chill, but that's not what grabbed our attention. It was the large, fluffy snowflakes falling from the sky, putting us in the middle of an actual glittering snow globe.

Emilia let out a shriek. "It's snowing! It's actually snowing."

"Ah! Alice, you were right. This day is just like a Christmas novel," Freddie said.

I nodded, awestruck, catching a snowflake on my tongue. It didn't usually snow in our village, and when it did, the snowflakes were never as large or as exquisite as these. They certainly didn't accumulate on the ground as quickly, either.

"Not a novel," Emilia said. "Home. It's just like home. Mom brought Boston to me." Emilia's eyes filled with happy tears, and Theo wiped each one away before they could venture past her nose.

"She did. And it's beautiful." I replied, looking at the sky. My attention was diverted when, beside me, Freddie tilted my face toward his. The light from the lamppost made each snowflake shimmer like confetti as it fell all around us. The moment felt magical.

"It is beautiful. Just like you, Alice." He leaned in closer, clearly about to kiss me. Did I want him to? I did. I absolutely did. My lips parted, welcoming his warmth. But before they met his, he pulled back.

"I can't."

My heart froze, and I prepared myself for the letdown when he grabbed my hand and pulled me a few steps over. "There," he said. "No mistletoe. I wanted to make it clear that I'm kissing you because I fancy you, Alice Evans, not because we are standing under a decorated lamppost."

Then, with anticipation bubbling inside me, his lips met mine. Soft and safe. Electrifying and sensual. The beginning of a beautiful something.

"Happy Christmas," he whispered into my ear.

"A happy Christmas, indeed," I replied before pulling his mouth back to mine and setting myself free.

Hi reader! I hope you enjoyed this little snippet into Alice's life. If you want to experience more of Berkingsley, pick up Emilia's story, titled *What's Handed Down*.

Reviews are a lifeline for authors. I would be forever grateful if you took the time to post a review on Goodreads, Instagram, and Amazon, and if you really loved it, tell your friends!

One of my favorite parts of being an author is connecting with other book lovers. Please find me on my socials and say hello!

Webpage: www.joellecullen.com
Instagram: @Joelle.cullen.author
Bookstagram: @Coffeeshopcorner
Facebook: JoelleCullenAuthor
TikTok: Joellecullenauthor
Email: Joelle.cullen.author@gmail.com

Acknowledgements

Wow, you're still reading! Thank you, thank you, thank you, reader, from the bottom of my heart. Without readers, an author's work is merely an imaginary story floating through her head. So many of you took a chance on me with my first novel, *What's Handed Down*, and for that, I'll be forever grateful. You've helped make my dreams come true. And you came back for a second story, which blows my mind even more! I hope this light, fun story brought joy to your life this holiday season.

By far, one of the best parts of being an author is connecting with other writers. Some have become such good friends and cheerleaders. I love you all. I'm talking to you... Valentina Burns, Jessica Booth, G.T. London, Kayla Martin, Nora Pritchard, Elizabeth Everett, Lauren Drew Martin, Emlynn Mcdermott, and C. D' Angelo.

Thank you to Another Chapter Bookstore for being one of the first stores to support my little book and to the local Barnes and Nobles for welcoming me with a smile and a Starbucks at my book signings.

I joke that my mom and mother-in-law are my marketing team because they are always telling everyone about my books. Thank you for your never-ending support. Love you both.

My first book-signing experience would not have been the amazing day it was without my lovely friends from college, high school, and motherhood, who all came out to support my first novel. You know who you are. Thank you.

To my kiddos: I love your enthusiasm for your mama's writing, from telling everyone you meet that your mom is an author to Blakey pointing to my book on the shelf and proclaiming in his baby voice, "That's Mama's book." It's a funny thing, but I'm glad I make you proud.

John: Thank you for supporting my dreams and for always giving me the window seat. I love you.

Finally, thank you, God, for all the people and experiences in life you have brought my way.

Also by Joelle Cullen

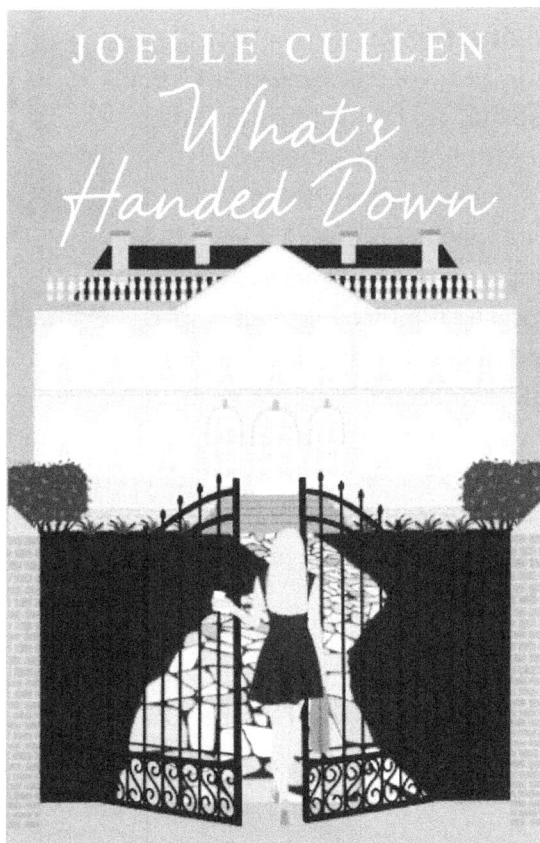

JOELLE CULLEN

What's Handed Down

Joelle Cullen

Women's Fiction with a side of Romance

Biography

Joelle Cullen has dreamt of becoming an author since she was a little girl. Following years of encouragement from her husband, she finally took the plunge into the author life in 2021. After many visits to the library paired with a white chocolate mocha latte (and a little help with supervision from her children's teachers), she finally completed her first novel set in her favorite place, London.

Joelle graduated summa cum laude from SUNY Geneseo and Syracuse University, with a BA in History and Education, and a MS in Special Education. She shared her love of history with hundreds of middle school students before staying home and raising her four children in Rochester, NY.

Now she spends her time writing, reviewing books on her bookstagram page, and shuttling her kids from activity to activity while singing Taylor Swift from the driver's seat. She might complain about the mess that gets made, but her kids and husband are the best parts of her life.

Made in United States
North Haven, CT
23 October 2024